THE GHOST WRITERS CLUB

A NOVEL

CODY WAYNE MORRIS

This book is for anyone who has been made to believe that the world doesn't need their art.

Yes it does.

PROLOGUE
LOGAN

Breathe in. Breathe out.

Those words consume my thoughts as I sit in the parking lot of Rosie's Diner. The cold night air burns my lungs, but it isn't nearly as bad as the smoke fighting its way out in the coughing fit that follows every exhale.

"You're doing great," declares an EMT, standing in the back of the ambulance. His voice is deep, and it has a gravel to it. I don't even turn to look at him, just stare at the ground. My legs dangle out over the pavement as I try to breathe calmly into the oxygen mask.

With each inhale, I attempt to take in more air, but every now and again, I get overzealous, which just leads to another coughing fit. My focus is so completely on my breathing that all of the commotion around me turns to static—the sirens, the scrambling footsteps, the police radios occasionally spouting random words and numbers, and the roar of the fire.

I look up from the gray pavement, moving my eyes to meet the diner. I can't help but marvel at the glow of the blaze against the black sky. Smoke pours from the windows and doors, draining the life from the place where I nearly lost mine—for the second time. I squint at the overwhelming brightness of the fire as if I'm looking directly into the sun.

The trucks and police cars arrived about ten minutes ago, and if not for them, my friends and I would still be inside, reduced to piles of smoldering ash. I watch as thick arches of water fall over the diner, hitting their mark with a sizzle until eventually the fire is gone, taking its light with it. The night is black again, broken only by the flashing red and blue lights and a couple of police cars with their headlights still on.

Breathe in. Breathe out.

I shift uncomfortably, the edge of the cold metal digging into the back of my thighs. I can feel my breathing become less and less strained. When I'm as close to normal as I'm going to get for the night, another EMT takes the mask from my face, exchanging it for a blanket over my shoulders to keep the chill out. The fabric is soft against my skin, the most comforting thing I've felt in the last twenty-four hours.

The nightmare is over. The initial shock seeps from my body, leaving an overwhelming sense of thankfulness and dread in its place. Tears fill my eyes and roll down my cheeks as I drop my head and sob.

A few minutes later, a hand touches my shoulder. I lift my head to see a woman in a police uniform taking a seat next to me. Her dark hair is tied in a tight knot behind her head, and her deep frown lines only accentuate her worried expression.

"Logan?" she asks, and I nod in response. "Do you think you can talk to me about what happened?" Her lips stretch to form a sympathetic smile, and though I have never met this woman, there's a warmth about her that, for an instant, makes me forget the prison of flames I managed to escape just moments ago.

I take a few more deep breaths, trying to calm my emotions, trying my best to piece my thoughts into sentences, but each time I play through tonight's events in my head, it's like reliving a nightmare over and over again.

I scan through my memories, searching for the moment where everything began. I watch the officer pull a small pen and notebook from her breast pocket, and my eyes follow the tip of her pen against the paper as she takes down my account of the evening.

- *Incident Report—Rosie's Diner—12:37 a.m.—Arson—Accident?*

When I see the last word—a question she wrote for herself—a chuckle escapes from my scratchy throat. I inhale deeply, then let out a long sigh, careful not to trigger another coughing fit.

"It's a long story," I warn.

"Take your time," she says, that warm smile returning to her face. "Just start at the beginning."

The beginning.

I can pinpoint the exact moment my life—my story—went spiraling toward everything that happened these last few months.

It starts and ends with the Ghost Writers Club.

I look back at the notepad, at the question the officer wrote to herself.

Accident?

That one question—that one word—could not be

further from the truth. The police don't know this yet, but the fire that nearly ended my life and left Rosie's Diner a pile of steam and ash was *anything* but an accident.

CHAPTER
ONE
LOGAN

THREE WEEKS EARLIER

I was so engrossed in setting up my dorm room after move-in day that I didn't notice the gathering crowd in the middle of Dorm Square.

In my opinion, the "square" is more like a rectangle, with four long stone buildings facing one another. In the center of it all is an old stone fountain depicting an angel, her wings tucked behind her back. She's holding a chalice in her outstretched hands, offering a drink to those who pass her by.

The sun set over an hour ago, and the alarm clock on my nightstand tells me it's almost nine. My stomach clamors, reminding me that I have yet to eat since the blueberry bagel and two eggs I had for breakfast. I was so focused on making sure everything was in order for my first day of classes tomorrow that I couldn't be bothered to stop and eat. My mom told me she wanted to send me off with a yummy breakfast, but I know what she was really doing.

She wanted to make one last effort to remind me just how good I have it at home. That everything I could ever want is there, and I can change my mind at any moment about coming to Westview. On her way out, she gave me a hug with tearful eyes and squeezed me just a little harder than normal.

"You know, home will always be a safe place for you to land," she whispered into my shirt, staining it with her tears.

I said nothing back. I just stood there and let her have her moment, because once it had passed, I would be free of her. I would never say this to my mom, but after everything that has happened over the last two years, there is only one thing I want more than fresh blueberry bagels and safety—freedom.

Only a few short hours ago, my mom was dropping me off here at Westview Writing Academy. Once we loaded everything into the room, she wanted to stay and help me unpack. When I told her I would take care of it, she protested, of course.

"Oh honey, please let me stay just a couple more hours! Who knows when I'll next see you."

To be honest, if I had given in and let her stay, I would have finished organizing my room hours ago. Well, it would have been more of me *trying* to organize and my mom going behind me and doing everything the "right" way.

There's a pile of clothes on my bed that I'll need to take care of before I tuck in for the night, but that will have to wait. I shift my weight on the padded bench built into the wall under the window and observe what looks like a candlelight service of some sort outside. A tall girl with bouncy auburn curls stands on the stone lip of the fountain's base, addressing the crowd, and even from my fourth-floor vantage point, I can see the tears streaming down her face.

Everyone in the crowd is holding a candle in their hand, their flames dancing from the slight breeze that sings through the marble arches built into the center of each building. Light trickles out onto the square from the surrounding dorm windows, and for a moment, I wonder if anyone else has taken interest in the service happening just outside.

Flowers adorn the lip of the fountain, and a large poster rests on an easel at the front of the crowd. On the poster is a picture of a girl. She has short, jet-black hair tousled on top of her head, and her eyes are a piercing blue like two pools filled with ice water. Her expression is . . . perplexing, to say the least. On the surface, she seems to be smiling, but the more I stare into those bright blue eyes, the more my mind begins to play tricks on me, like she's some sort of modern-day Mona Lisa.

While I never met her, I recognize her as Lexi Pruitt, the girl whose death shook Westview and the surrounding cities. She was the daughter of a famous lawyer, Jeff Pruitt, who made a name for himself representing the underdog. When the news broke that Lexi had taken her own life, people speculated about how different she'd been after losing her father. I wonder how long they'd had that realization and just kept it to themselves. If they knew she was hurting, why wait until it was too late to say something? Maybe if they had, she would be here to tell her own story, instead of being reduced to a picture on an easel surrounded by people who never bothered to speak to her when she was alive.

I wish I could hear what they were saying about her. I

move my hands to the latches above the window, but upon further inspection, the edges have been sealed shut.

I trace the perimeter with my finger, and I can't help but wonder what would prompt such a precaution.

They say 95 percent of rules are made for 5 percent of people. My dad's words echo in my mind.

Were the sealed windows meant to keep others *out*, or to ensure that we stay *in*?

One of the things I was most excited about with having a room on the fourth floor was being able to allow fresh air in and to watch people from my perch. I suppose I can still do the latter, but what good is watching them if I can't hear what they're talking about?

I have always taken an interest in listening to others. My father used to tell me that every person we encounter has a story of their own to tell. He found himself fascinated with these stories. So much so, in fact, that he made a name for himself telling the stories of those the world has discarded—murderers.

It's actually because of my dad that I even ended up at Westview in the first place. Though this is my first time attending as a student, I've walked this campus many times before.

For as long as I can remember, my dad was someone I looked up to. He attended Westview back in the late nineties, and while he was here, his goal was to make a name for himself. He was the first in his family to go to college, and it was on this very campus where he met my mom. I've heard the story countless times growing up. My dad was sitting in the library, working on the first draft of what he hoped would be his debut novel, when the most beautiful woman he had ever seen walked into his view.

"I must have been staring," my dad would say, trying

to hold back one of his boisterous laughs, "because when your mom locked eyes with me, she just smiled and placed the back of her hand under her chin. I was so entranced that I didn't realize she was telling me to close my mouth, which at the time had fallen to the floor."

The story always ended with my dad leaning over to tell my mother how beautiful she was and reminding her that she only grew more beautiful with each passing day. My parents got married two weeks after graduating from Westview Writing Academy, and the rest is history. Typically, I cringed every time my dad told this story, but now that he's gone, I would give anything to hear him tell it one last time.

My dad always found a fascination in the psyches of those who society has labeled as "criminal." He wanted to get to the root of the human condition, and believed that people are born innately good—even killers. He made it his mission to get to the source of what led these people down a path that ended with spending the rest of their life behind bars. He sought to question the morality of murder if one has no other option.

"If villains can have a tragic backstory to explain all of their wrongdoings, why can't we?" he would say.

His fascination only grew from there, and he took it upon himself to tell their stories. He would spend hours in his office, searching for potential candidates in an attempt to set up interviews with them. Some were more willing to talk than others, and the ones who did talk were glad they had.

When the first installment of *Chronicles of a Killer* came out, it was an instant hit. People all over the world were reading my dad's book. As a result, the subjects began to receive an outpouring of love from their communities—

letters, flowers, and sometimes even money to be used toward their legal fees. In the letters, fans would note how much courage it required for these people to take their lives back into their own hands. Some fans even stated that under similar circumstances, they would have done the same.

My dad went on to publish volume after volume, and with each new release, his fan base grew. After the third installment, he was being booked for radio shows and TV appearances, which my mom diligently recorded on the DVR. We held a watch party for my dad's first TV appearance, and when he got home from the studio, he decided to celebrate by pouring a glass of whiskey on the rocks and sitting with his notepad to take notes on how he could improve for his next interview. That's the kind of man my dad was—always seeking to be better than he was the day before. That is how I will remember him. That is his legacy.

I watch out my window as the candlelight service comes to a close. The crowd begins to thin as, one by one, each person makes their way out of the courtyard, taking a little piece of light with them. After another few moments filled with tearful hugs, the pavilion grows dark again and the angel standing in the fountain is nothing more than a shadow. Most of the light that once poured from the other dorms is now absent, which means most everyone has tucked in for the night in preparation for the first day of classes tomorrow. I glance again at the clock, which now shows a little after ten.

I stand from the window and stretch my arms toward the ceiling, stifling a yawn as I take in the progress I made today. My desk is set up with a fresh set of notebooks and pens; my video games and movies now line the shelf that sits under the TV. My books have all been unpacked and placed on a bookshelf that I bought for cheap and refurbished this past summer. There are still a few boxes stacked against the wall next to the thick wooden door, but those will have to be tomorrow's problem.

I take a quick minute to pull the clothes from my bed and place them in the chest of drawers that are fastened to the floor of the closet and hang up my nicer shirts and pants so they don't get creased or wrinkled. I do this until there is only one article of clothing left—a dark blue zip-up jacket.

To anyone else, the jacket would be just a plain thing, but to me, it is one of the last things I have that belonged to my dad. The deep blue of the fabric has faded from years of washing, and there are a couple of frays on the cuff of the right sleeve. My mom begged my dad to throw it away and even took it upon herself to buy him a new one, but he just couldn't seem to part with it. He wrote his first book wearing that jacket. After that, he wore it every time he sat down to write, and he believed that if he threw it away, all of his inspiration and success would go with it.

When he died of cancer over two years ago, my mom let me pick something of his to remember him by. I immediately went into his office and grabbed the jacket from the back of his chair, where he'd left it the last time he sat down to write.

I lift it from the bed and press the soft fabric of the jacket to my face. I breathe deeply, taking the scent into my nose. It smells like home—like a happier time, when my dad was still here. I unzip the jacket and slide my arms into the sleeves to pull it over my shoulders, and immediately all of the hustle and bustle of the move today melts away.

I pull the sheets back and crawl into bed, then flip the

switch on the wall above my bed, and the room goes dark. Lying there with my eyes closed, I'm filled with anticipation of the first day at a new school. There's also the inevitable pressure that I bear with my last name—I don't plan to waste the chance to show the world what Leonard Clark's son can do.

When my dad started to get sick, he told me that he wished he could have written just one more book, and I promised him that I would be sure to write his last book in his honor.

If anyone can do it, it's you, Logan. His words echo again.

My thoughts swirl around me as I lie there in the dark. Tomorrow is a new beginning, where I will gain the tools I need to write the book my dad and his fan base can be proud of.

One final thought passes through my mind as I drift off to sleep.

Step one: I need to find a killer.

CHAPTER
TWO
LOGAN

The nightmare always ends with a blinding light.

The beginning, at least from what I can remember, starts with darkness, the world around me flipped on its head. Jagged lines cover my field of view, like looking through a broken kaleidoscope.

A pressure builds in my skull, and my hand flies to my pulsing temple—or at least it tries to. I look to my arm, which is pinned to my side by some invisible force. I can wiggle my fingers, but my limb feels like it's been gorilla glued there. My other arm moves to assist, but I soon realize that it too is being held in place.

I'm trapped.

My body convulses, attempting to break free of whatever is binding me, but it's no use. Suddenly, there's a flicker of light. It grows in size and intensity, revealing a human-shaped shadow strolling in my direction.

"Hello!" I call out to it. "I'm stuck. I need help!"

The shadow doesn't speak. It moves closer to me, its feet scraping against the ground with every step. The scraping grows louder until the noise is unbearable, like nails grating on a chalkboard. I want to cover my ears, but arms remain in place, ignoring my every command.

I force my eyes closed, and with every ounce of will I can muster, I scream, "Stop!"

I'm unsure who or what I am screaming at, but it does.

My eyes fall open in surprise. The only sound is the one still ringing in my ears and—is that mumbling? I look to the shadow, which now stands motionless ten feet from me. I can't make out their face, but I concentrate on where their mouth should be. There's a rhythm to their words, as if they're repeating the same thing on a loop. I listen a while, attempting to sound out what they're saying, but inevitably give up.

A light flickers in the sky to my right. I turn to face it, looking for the source, but there isn't one. It's like watching a shooting star, only this one is growing and—I swallow hard—it's heading right at me.

"Please! You have to help me," I call to the shadow.

Panic rises in my chest, and I use every ounce of strength I possess to fight against my invisible restraints. I claw, and I yank, and I pull, but nothing works.

Suddenly, the shadow that was standing ten feet away mere seconds ago has now teleported to my side. Long, spindly fingers creep up my neck and force my eyelids open. My head turns to face the light, and I realize that whoever or whatever this thing is, they are forcing me to watch my last seconds alive.

The shadow continues to mumble, only now I can make out every word.

You deserve to die. You deserve to die. You deserve to die.

A scream rips from my throat as the nightmare burns into blinding white light.

I sit up in the bed, my clothes damp against my cold skin. I was hopeful that coming to Westview and having a fresh start would lessen the frequency of the nightmares, but clearly that is not going to be the case.

My body is stiff as I toss away the covers and place my feet on the cold tile floor. The cold is soothing against my sore bones. Since the accident, my body has a hard time recovering from physical labor. I tilt my head from side to side to release the tension in my neck until the stiffness subsides. I do the same with my shoulders, working down my body to my ankles and toes.

It's an exercise my physical therapist referred to as "top-down stretching," where I allow each part of my body the opportunity to warm up before standing. It's times like these I am so grateful to not have a roommate, because I look like the tin man in *The Wizard of Oz*, oiling up each joint until my body cooperates.

I look at the clock, which tells me I have about an hour until my first class—plenty of time to get ready and grab a coffee beforehand. I stand from the bed, allowing gravity to press on my sore joints. In thirty minutes, I'm out the door, and in another ten or so, I'm standing in line at the coffee shop. I'm not in line for very long before the hair on the back of my neck stands at attention.

I'm being watched.

I turn to look toward the entrance to Coleman Hall, where students are now arriving in flocks. This building is the main hub for the fresh meat on campus, as most of the first-year classes are held here. I scan each face, looking for the culprit, but come up short. As far as I can tell, no one here has taken notice of me, and I'd like for it to stay that way.

"Logan!" One of the baristas shouts my name over the noise of bustling students. I walk over and retrieve my coffee, and as I turn to head to my first class, I feel a hand on my shoulder.

I jump, nearly throwing my coffee to the ground. My body whips around to face the older woman standing behind me. Her silver-speckled hair is up in a clip behind her head, and she's staring back at me through a pair of turquoise glasses that match the rest of her ensemble.

"I'm so sorry. I didn't mean to startle you," she says, her face wrinkling with worry.

"That's alright," I say, finding my breath.

"My name is Deborah Smith, but you can call me Debbie. You're Logan Clark, correct?"

I nod. I should have expected that it wouldn't take long for someone to recognize me. After all, I'm the son of one of the most notable alumni this school has ever known. I was hoping to keep a low profile on the first day, but apparently I've already failed in that regard.

"Oh splendid!" she says, her worry replaced by a wide smile. "It's such an honor to meet one of Westview's most anticipated legacies. Dean Aldridge would like to meet with you before your first class begins. May I escort you to his office?"

I hesitate for a moment. I mean, I literally just walked into the door, and the dean is already wanting to meet with me? So much for keeping a low profile.

"Sure," I say with forced enthusiasm, looking around to make sure no one else is paying attention to this exchange. I turn back to Deborah, who's already a few steps away from where she was standing just a few seconds ago.

"This way, dear." She waves her arm, gesturing for me to follow her. And so I do.

"Dean Aldridge is just finishing up his last meeting this morning. Take a seat and I'll let him know you've stopped by."

Stopped by? Deborah makes it sound like I wasn't just hunted down at a coffee shop and asked to follow her here. Regardless, I do as she says and take a seat in one of the four leather chairs outside the office door. A sigh escapes me as I sink further into the seat, which to my surprise is much more comfortable that it looks.

On the wall opposite of me, I notice a bulletin board adorned with a colorful array of papers with large, dramatic font choices. Flyers for all of the social groups on campus—Shakespeare's Soirée, Founding Fathers of Fiction, Writers Realm, and so many more. Only one catches my attention.

The flyer is barren, flaunting only a QR code printed in black ink. They didn't put any words on it or even bother to print it on colorful paper. What kind of club advertises with just plain white copy paper?

I stand from the leather chair to get a better view. As I approach the flyer, I can see now that the QR code is in the shape of a skull.

Okay. Now I'm intrigued.

I reach into my pocket to pull out my phone, opening it to the camera app to scan the skull. Just as the page begins to pull up, the door to the dean's office swings open.

"Thanks for stopping by, Julia. Give my best to Chief Scott," Deborah says to the girl leaving the office before locking eyes with me. "Logan, thank you so much for being patient. It should only be another minute." She waves before retreating back through the door.

"So *you're* the Logan I've been hearing so much about," the girl says, tucking her short brown hair behind her ear.

Damn it. I guess word travels fast with Deborah.

"My name is Julia," she adds. "Were you looking at some of the clubs on campus?"

I look back at the bulletin board, then down to my phone, which is still loading the website scanned from the QR code. These buildings are old, so I'm not surprised to see that there's hardly a signal in here.

Note to self: Log on to the campus Wi-Fi when I get to my first class.

"What can you tell me about this one?" My finger points to the skull-shaped QR code on the wall.

"Ooooo, the Ghost Writers Club. Interesting choice."

"What's that?" I ask.

"They're a band of rogue writers who felt like they didn't fit in any of the other clubs. So, they decided to start one of their own."

"Oh, well that sounds nice," I say naively.

"Yeah. Too bad no one knows who they are."

"What do you mean?"

"I mean, they're sort of a secret society. No one knows who's in the club, and they like to keep it that way. They report on the things the campus doesn't want to get out like they're some sort of self-proclaimed truth seekers."

"So it's basically a gossip blog?"

"I guess you could say that, but the stuff they've posted has definitely made them some enemies."

"Is the stuff they post on their blog true?"

Julia looks at the flyer on the wall and back to me before shrugging her shoulders.

"I don't know, but I guess if people believe it, then it becomes true to them. That alone will keep anyone coming

back to your blog. They posted pretty regularly until— "
Julia stops, as if to contemplate her next few words.

"Until what?" I ask, my curiosity piqued.

Her voice is a near whisper. "The incident with Lexi."

Silence falls between us, leaving space for me to process the weight of her words.

"Incident?"

Julia's hazel eyes remain locked on mine, and a solemn expression flashes across her face, leaving as quickly as it appears.

"Oh yeah. It happened last summer. All I really know about it is what I've seen in the paper or from random speculation on campus. I don't know if you saw, but they actually held a memorial service for her last night in Dorm Square."

Suddenly, my thoughts go back to the scene I witnessed just outside my dorm room last night. The service was for a girl named Lexi, and it clicks. *Lexi was a Ghost Writer.*

"Oh, I did see that. Did you know her?" I ask, prompting another momentary slip of Julia's expression. Her lips tighten as she takes in a pinched breath, releasing it with a long sigh before she speaks again.

"We had a couple classes together. Other than that, we didn't hang out much." She forces a grin, but I see right through it.

Julia and I just met, so she doesn't know how good I am at detecting a lie. I learned a lot about body language from my dad, who would interview potential candidates for his next book, and within about ten minutes, he would know if they were telling the truth or not.

The flash of emotion on Julia's face was a dead give-away that she knows more than she's letting on. "Incident" to me sounds like there may have been other forces involved in her death, and if that's the case, the Ghost Writers may be a good starting place to find my killer, and tell their story.

Julia and I are silent for a moment longer, until the door to the dean's office opens. We both turn to see Deborah peeking her head out with a toothy grin.

"Logan, the dean will see you now," she says, waving me toward her.

I give her a nod and drop my phone in my pocket before collecting my things from the leather chair. I throw my bag over my shoulder, and when I turn back to Julia, she's checking her watch.

"I need to go and grab some coffee before my first class. It was nice to meet you, Logan," Julia says with an outstretched hand. I take her hand in mine, and she leans closer to me to speak in a hushed tone. "Word on the street is, the Ghost Writers are planning their big comeback this year."

My eyes widen, and I turn to face the QR skull. I look at it the same way a hungry dog looks at a ribeye, my mouth nearly salivating with curiosity.

Deborah clears her throat, signaling to me that I need to hurry this conversation along.

"I'll see you around Logan," Julia says, dropping my hand. She walks down the hallway, her knee-length sunflower skirt flowing behind her. I look back at the bulletin board, almost as if it's calling out to me. Whispering welcomes—or warnings, it's too early to tell—into my ears.

One thought solidifies as I step into Dean Aldridge's office:

I need to find out more about the Ghost Writers Club.

CHAPTER
THREE
LOGAN

I plop onto my bed after an exhausting first day of classes. It wasn't exhausting mentally—each of my professors pretty much just spent ten minutes going over the syllabus before turning us loose to wait for our next class. I swear, sometimes I think the first day of classes should be an email. They could have just as easily sent their syllabi to us and let us review them in our pajamas from the comfort of our own beds.

After a few minutes of lying on my back, I can feel the tension leaving the bottoms of my feet. Living at home with a mom to aid my every beck and call, I didn't get around much. Most of my walks consisted of going to the bathroom or moving from the bed to the couch. Toward the end of my recovery, I started taking strolls around our neighborhood. I would tell my mom that it was good for me to build my endurance up before coming to Westview, since my main mode of transportation around campus would be walking. Truthfully, I just wanted an excuse to get out of the house and away from her watchful eye.

Speaking of my mom, when I dig my phone from my pocket, I see three new text messages have appeared on my lock screen.

> Hey sweetie! Hope you had the most amazing first day!
>
> I miss you so much already!
>
> Did you like your new teachers?

I stare at the blinking cursor. After another moment, I hold down the second message and heart-react to it before typing my response.

> First day was good. Teachers were nice.
>
> Going to finish setting up my room and then I'm headed to bed.
>
> Talk to you later. Love you.

Once the last message is sent, I close out of the app and tap on the web browser. It opens up to the website I scanned from the QR code this morning. The webpage is pretty barren. A replica of the blocky skull from the flier sits in the middle of the page above a black rectangle that reads *ATTACH SUBMISSION HERE* in bright red letters.

I reload the page a few times, hoping that more information will populate, but nothing does. I copy the link and text it to myself before opening my laptop. Once I log in, the text appears on the top right of my screen, and I click on the link. I hold my breath, waiting for the page to load, only to find that it's identical to the one on my phone—barren.

I was hoping there would at least be some sort of instructions on what I'm supposed to write about, but there isn't anything here to convince me that this group is even real. I flop my laptop on the bed in frustration and close my eyes.

The conversation I had with Julia this morning comes back to me. For some reason, she thinks that the Ghost Writers are going to be making their big comeback this year. Her words echo in my mind.

"They report on the things the campus doesn't want to get out like they're some sort of self-proclaimed truth seekers."

I've always thought of my dad as a truth seeker. He made a career of telling the stories of others and, in a way, sought to expose the truth about all of the things wrong with society. He blamed elected officials for creating an environment where the subjects of his books had no other choice but to turn to a life of crime in order to survive. Sure, he received hate, but it never fazed him. Or, at least, I never *saw* it faze him.

Suddenly, I know exactly what I want to write about in my submission. There's no way to know if what I write will meet their criteria, but if they wanted something different, they should have specified it on their website. I grab my laptop and open a blank Word document and start typing.

———

I'll never forget the first time my heart felt like it was actually broken. When my dad was diagnosed with stage four cancer, we knew that his time was limited. I had to watch someone I considered invincible wither away before my very eyes. Every day brought a new challenge that my dad couldn't face on his own, and as his body died, so too did the light behind his eyes.

He would fight constantly when my mom would try to help

him get around the house. It wasn't until he physically couldn't care for himself that he finally gave in to her. He had no other choice.

It hurts badly enough to watch someone you care about slip through the cracks; I can only imagine how he must have felt to be trapped in a body that failed him more and more each day. All he could do was watch and wait for death to come take him away.

The day of my dad's funeral was the day I finally came to terms with the fact that he was gone. I had spent so much time while he was sick consoling my mother that I never actually took the time to mourn my own loss. When we arrived at the church where his service was to be held, I stayed close to my mom. I knew there would be an onslaught of friends and family that I hadn't seen in years. She took the brunt of the greeting, and I would shake hands with them or accept their hugs with a forced smile.

Before the service started, the young lady who was running it allowed my mom and me to have a minute alone with him to say goodbye. The man I saw in the casket was just a shadow of who my dad had been. His face resembled my dad's, but everything else about him was foreign to me. My mom went up to the casket first and sobbed so loud, I was certain that the neighboring town could hear. She composed herself and looked back to me, reaching out a hand to invite me forward.

I took my place next to her. She placed her hand on my back, and something inside of me shattered. All of the feelings I had been pushing away were now bubbling to the surface, and there was nothing I could do to stop it. I fell to my knees and sobbed. I don't know how long I had been down there before the young lady came back into the room to let us know it was time to take him.

"No!" I yelled, catching everyone, including myself, off guard. "You can't take him!"

I held on to the casket for dear life, shutting my tear-filled eyes to pray to whatever higher power would listen.

Please don't take my dad from me. Please.

I would have said anything, prayed to any god, if it meant my dad would open his eyes again. If they could grant me one last time to have my dad tell me it was all going to be okay.

I found my composure and steadied myself back to my feet. My eyes burned from the salty tears, and when I finally allowed myself to step away, I shot the young lady a look and apologized for yelling at her.

She gave me a gentle, understanding nod before she and her assistant stepped toward the casket and sealed it shut. As they rolled him out of the room and into the sanctuary, I felt like a piece of me had been taken and sealed in that wooden box with him and was now being rolled away for the last time.

Everything about the service was beautiful. On the stage, behind the speaker, was a forest of flowers from friends, family, and strangers I had never met. The sanctuary was standing-room only, and as I looked around, I realized something. Every bouquet of flowers that surrounded my father's casket represented a life that had been made better simply because he was a part of it.

I scan over my submission a few more times, making small edits here and there. I made sure not to make any mention of who my dad was. I don't want to be accepted into a club on the basis of my last name and the weight that comes with it.

My mouse hovers over the black rectangle. This could be the start of my story here at Westview. While I may be putting myself in danger, it will be worth it, because in the end, I'll be able to write the book that ends my father's legacy and starts my own.

Before I can talk myself out of it, I click on the button, and my submission leaves the screen. Now it's in the hands of the Ghost Writers, whoever they may be.

I shut my laptop and notice how quiet my room is. The constant noise of water rushing through the fountain outside my window has stopped, letting me know that the sun has set. I peek out through the blinds and into the courtyard. All of the rest of the students have returned to their dorms, and the angel stands in the fountain, staring back at me through the shadows.

I'd like to think that she's watching over me now that I'm here alone. I look at my phone, eager to see a message come across my screen, but it's late, and whoever is on the other side of that submission box has probably tucked in for the night. I toss my phone to the side and jump to my feet to get ready for bed.

An hour later, I'm crawling under the sheet completely spent from the day. I feel something hard under me and pull my phone from under the sheets. I tap on the screen to check the time, and when it comes to life, my breath catches in my lungs.

A new email, from an unknown sender. I open it and wait in anticipation. When it finally loads, I read the message.

Logan Reeves,

Old Library. Tomorrow. 10pm.

–GWC

My eyes can't believe what they're seeing. I don't know if I should respond, or just show up as instructed. My mind spirals, and I think to myself that there's no way that I can go to sleep now. I read the email one last time before locking my phone and placing it on the wireless charger that sits on my nightstand.

I flip the light switch above my head, and darkness shrouds the room. In the still silence, I can hear my heart beating in my ears. I breathe in deeply through my nose and out of my mouth. I do this a few times until the excitement melts away, leaving behind the fatigue I felt just moments ago.

Tomorrow, I am going to meet the Ghost Writers Club.

CHAPTER
FOUR
LOGAN

"Logan!"

Professor Alexander's boisterous voice echoes throughout the auditorium. I slam my phone down on the table in front of me, quickly moving my eyes to meet my professor's.

"Would you like to add anything?"

I stare deeply into his emerald eyes as I scrounge through the recesses of my mind. I have no idea what subject was being discussed just a few moments ago, and the longer my classmates bore their gazes into me, the more blood I can feel rushing to my cheeks.

"Perhaps Mr. Reeves should pay closer attention when he is in my class."

A few giggles break out across the room as I slouch as low as I can in my seat. Any lower, and I would be a puddle on the floor.

By the end of class, the pain from my public shaming has numbed slightly, and I make a beeline for the door. I'm nearly at freedom when I hear that boisterous voice calling out my name once again.

I freeze before stepping out of the way of other students. Once a majority have made their way through the double doors, I walk back down the steps toward Professor Alexander.

The closer I get, the more I feel like I should be the first to say something. I was on my phone in class, and I should be the one to apologize, but I can't seem to let myself say the words. I take in a shaky breath of air to speak, but he beats me to it.

"Your father was a good friend of mine." He packs his laptop and a stack of papers into his satchel. "He was an even better writer. We all knew he would be the one to make it big out of our group. You know . . ." He lets out a low chuckle. "I used to envy your dad's success, but when I saw all of the publicity he had to deal with—" He clicks the buckles on his satchel. "Let's just say, I wasn't made for the limelight. Too much pressure to be perfect all the time. I would have caved after the first year, but your dad was stronger than all of us."

Hearing Professor Alexander speak of my father in such high regard is not the conversation I expected after being called out in front of the entire class. I try to think of something to say, but the words are held down by the knot forming in my throat.

"You have been given a great opportunity, but also a great responsibility. Best not to waste it with frivolous distractions," he says, flicking his gaze down to the phone in my hand.

I give an understanding nod. "I'm sorry, Professor. It won't happen again."

He smiles as he throws his satchel over his shoulder,

and I turn to start for the doors in the back of the auditorium. I make it about halfway before he speaks again.

"Westview is easy to get lost in. Once people know who you are, they will try to befriend you. Some will see your heart. Some will see you as an opportunity. Do try your best to learn which is which."

I turn back once more. "Thank you, Professor."

Then I hold my breath until I finally cross the threshold out of the auditorium.

Following my last class of the day, I take the long way back to my dorm. I walk across the campus, which is bustling with students making their way to enjoy whatever plans they've laid out for the evening. I keep walking, making sure to keep my head down. After the events of the week so far, the last thing I want right now is another person to tell me how much pressure I should or should not feel being here at Westview. My pace slows as my destination comes into view.

The old library is somewhat of a monument on Westview's campus. Tall stone walls with snakes of ivy growing along them in all directions. An array of red and yellow tulips line the front of the building, shaded by two small trees framing the entrance. It's nice to see that after all this time, the exterior has been well kept.

When the new library was constructed in the center of campus, the Walker-Williams Library—now referred to plainly as the "Old Library"—slowly transformed from a place filled with books, readers, and daydreaming writers to a vacant shell of its former self. It became a place to host social gatherings and events, each room with its own pieces of history to gawk at. Even now the building seems . . . sad somehow. As if it too knows that it will never serve its intended purpose again.

. . .

About eight years ago, Westview's board made plans to demolish the Old Library to make space for more amenities on campus. This was not well-received among locals, and when Mayor Flores caught wind of it, he used his large following to keep it from happening.

He organized a strike to take place during the forty-eight hours before it was planned to be torn down. Citizens and alumni alike flocked to campus to protect a place that held so many fond memories for them.

I remember standing on the steps of the library between my mom and dad. They both held signs protesting the tearing down of the place where their love story began. They made a smaller sign for me even though, at twelve years old, I was already taller than my mom. My dad had even sent out the flyer about the protest in one of his newsletters. There must have been at least a hundred of his readers there, prepared to go to war for his cause.

Though it was supposed to be a forty-eight-hour strike, the sheer amount of support for the event was astounding. The board made the unanimous decision to cease the teardown of the structure in just five short hours.

When the announcement was made, everyone cheered and hugged one another with tears of joy speckling our faces. The Old Library was deemed a monument of the city and was to be kept up by the community. Its gothic look makes it a great venue for events, but when it wasn't booked, it lay empty.

Why would the Ghost Writers want to meet in a place like this?

I look at the large wooden doors, and my attention is drawn to the chain wrapped around the metal door handles. A sign mounted to the door reads *NO TRESPASS-ING. VIOLATORS WILL BE PROSECUTED.*

Suddenly, a queasy feeling fills the pit of my stomach. Here I am at a brand new school, and already, I feel like there are eyes following me everywhere I go. It's probably not the best idea to start my story here at Westview with slapping a criminal charge on my permanent record. Maybe I read the email wrong? This club can't possibly be having me risking the law to join their group, can they? I pull my phone from my pocket and click on the email.

Logan Reeves,

Old Library. Tomorrow. 10pm.

–GWC

Nope. This is definitely the place.

The sound of clanging metal erupts from the left side of the building. My head jolts toward the noise, and my body tenses. Maybe one of the Ghost Writers is hanging around the building, and if I'm quiet enough, I can catch a glimpse of them.

I walk down the sidewalk until I reach the corner of the building. A path of green grass separates the tall brick wall and a small forest of dense trees. It leads down a hill to where a small stream of water runs from an underground tunnel closed off by an iron gate. I sneak down the hill, keeping my eyes on the trees and checking for any sign of movement. At the bottom, I look through the metal gate and see a path of mud and water that disappears into dark nothingness.

My shoulders slouch in disappointment. Perhaps it was only a normal maintenance worker doing their normal maintenance job. Boring.

I climb back up the hill and return to my place on the sidewalk. I take one last look at the building, again taking note of the sign that reads more like a threat. I swallow hard, forcing down the anxiety I feel surrounding tonight, and start walking toward my dorm.

———

I toss and turn in my bed. Just when I feel like I'm happy with my decision to not go tonight, a little voice in the back of mind creeps up and taunts me.

Aren't you a little curious?

Obviously, I am more than a little curious, and while my mission is to look for a killer, I would prefer that I not become a victim in the process.

I look over at the clock, which now reads 9:40. If I left now, I would arrive at the Old Library just before ten. Maybe I could just walk past the library. You can't be prosecuted for trespassing if you never *actually* trespass. Besides, some fresh air can't hurt.

The weather this time of year is the kind where you can wear shorts and a T-shirt during the day, but once the sun starts to set, you need to add some layers. I grab my dad's blue jacket from the bed and begin to slide my arms into the sleeves. As I zip it up, I glance out of my window to the angel fountain. When the sun is high in the sky, her presence feels like I have a protective guardian, but when I look at her in the dark, she seems to be warning me, asking me to use caution should I leave her sight.

As I walk across campus, the chilled air whips between buildings, shaking the leaves from their branches overhead. With each step I take toward the library, I can feel my heart pounding in my ears.

Why am I so nervous?

I'm not even sure I'll be going inside the library, but for

some reason, walking toward the unknown feels more thrilling than terrifying.

Professor Alexander's words ring in my ears, how some will see me as an opportunity.

If only I had received that warning before I outright told a group of mystery writers who I was. What if this is some sort of trap? They could be waiting in the wings for me to walk into the library and have the authorities on speed dial. Such a small moment in time can make or break me here at Westview, and I can't take that risk.

The lampposts that stand on either side of the building have a pitiful glow, barely lighting the ground below them. The library itself stands like a shadow against the night sky. I stop on the sidewalk just in front of the Old Library, scanning for obvious places someone could be hiding, waiting for me to make a wrong move. I'm about to turn away when a small flicker of light catches my eye, just in front of the door. I squint slightly and lean forward, trying to understand what I'm looking at. My eyes widen when I realize that the rusted chain that was wrapped around the handles before is now gone—and the right-hand door is slightly propped open.

My gaze falls back to the flickering light, and I realize that a candle had been placed on the front stoop, its flame dancing in the breeze that occasionally blows between the buildings. I cross my arms over my chest to try and keep the wind from piercing through both layers of clothing. When the gust subsides, I lift my face to look around me. The campus is a ghost town filled only by the sounds of night creatures and rustling leaves that cover the ground in a blanket of orange and red. I listen carefully. Anyone walking close enough to see me would reveal themselves with the sound of leaves shuffling underfoot.

Nothing.

I look back to the flickering candle and the door that begs to usher me in. Maybe I'm being paranoid. I let Professor Alexander's words get to me, and I was just making up scenarios in my head. If this is where the group calls home, then they must have gotten some sort of permission to operate out of this building. Besides, if anything happens, I can just play the "new kid who didn't know any better" card.

I have to do this. If not for myself, then for my dad. I know if he were in my shoes, he wouldn't hesitate to march inside, consequences be damned. He would risk everything to get to the truth. I wish every day I could be more like him and less like my mother, who weighs every outcome multiple times before making a decision.

I take one last look around, and once I deem the coast clear, I take a deep breath and start for the entrance.

CHAPTER
FIVE
LOGAN

he heavy doors howl as I push them open. I retrieve the candle from the stoop and hold it out in front of me in an attempt to light the dark entrance. Then I step inside, allowing the door to close behind me, though I make sure it remains slightly ajar in case I need a quick exit. I turn to step farther in, letting my eyes adjust, and I realize I am standing in the foyer. To my right sits a large desk covered with stationary and a single computer monitor.

The room itself looks pristine, all dark tiled floors and long drapes cast down the length of the tall windows. A stale sort of smell fills the space. It's the kind you would expect in a building this old, with books of the same age or older.

I linger for a moment before my attention is drawn to a glow behind the desk. I tiptoe around it and find another candle has been placed on the floor.

No. Not just one candle. A trail of them leads down the main hall of the building. I follow their path and see that they stop just before another large door with a circle window in the center of it.

I step down the hallway, holding my candle close to my chest. The walls are lined with portraits of famous writers of the past—Edgar Allen Poe, Shakespeare, Emily Dickinson—each boring their eyes into me as I pass by.

I approach the door at the end of the hall and, from the glow of my candle, see the same skull from the flyer outside Dean Aldridge's office.

This is it.

My mind races through all of the possibilities of what could be on the other side of this door. If this is a trap of some kind, I will know in a matter of a few more steps forward. I could just as easily turn around and run out of here the way I came in, but I know that I would drive myself mad thinking of what could have come from this.

I close my eyes and fidget with the sleeve of my jacket. I don't know if he can hear me, but I hope that my dad is somehow watching over me and guiding me to make the right decision.

I push open the door, and my mouth falls open. I remember this room from a few book-signing events I attended with my dad. When I saw it for the first time, I couldn't believe how many books there were.

"Finite resources. Infinite knowledge," my dad would say each time we entered the circular room.

We were set up at a table surrounded by floor-to-ceiling bookshelves, all filled to the brim with books from all genres and time periods. To the right of the room was a grand marble fireplace framed by two lion statues. Couches and ornate chairs had once formed a seating area around it, and near that was a shelf dedicated to books written by alumni of the college. I made it a point to run over to see my dad's books on the shelves. I would count how many were missing and thought it was the coolest thing ever that somewhere on campus, there were students reading his stories.

He loved this library and spent many hours of his life working and writing within these walls, but seeing it now, I realize it's a mere skeleton of what it once was.

The towering shelves lie bare, devoid of the stories they once shared. The marble fireplace is ablaze with a fresh fire, its orange glow filling the room and dancing along the walls. The furniture that resided in front of the fireplace has been stripped down to a single ornate red chair sitting and facing the flames.

I'm the only one here as far as I can tell, so I can only assume that the chair is meant for me. As I move closer to the fireplace, I glance around the first floor and the balconies overhead, searching for any sign that I'm not alone. I look back to the chair and notice that the word *SIT* has been painted in blood-red across the back. A blank piece of white paper and a marker are lying on the seat of the chair, and I lift them before taking my place.

The chair is surprisingly comfortable, and I sink deep into the cushion, leaning against the soft back, which stops just above my head. I get lost in the flames until I hear a large door opening and closing behind me. My body goes stiff as footsteps echo throughout the hollow room.

My thoughts beg me to turn around, but my body refuses to cooperate as the sound grows closer, stopping just behind me. A moment of silence stretches before the first voice rings out.

"Welcome," the voice calls, bouncing from wall to wall. "So you have come to join us, have you?"

"This club," a softer voice follows, "is a group of prestigious minds who have come together to create one writer. No one individual holds more weight or power over their fellow colleague. No one individual receives acclaim to their name alone. We are all cogs that work to operate the one machine. If one cog does not hold their own, the entire machine fails. Do you accept these terms?"

I squirm in the chair. I've seen movies about some of the rituals involved with fraternities and sororities, but living it feels like an out-of-body experience. After a moment of silence, I answer with a shaky breath. "Uh—" I clear my dry throat. "Yes, I do."

"Very well," a third voice replies, this one familiar in some way. "Now, you must release yourself of your own individual identity. Outside of these walls, you are Logan, but within these walls, in the presence of your fellow colleagues, you are one part of the whole brain. Please write your name on the piece of paper provided."

I grab for the marker that has somehow wedged itself between my left leg and the arm of the chair. Silence fills the room as I remove the cap and spell my name in large red letters across the page.

"Take one last look at your name," the third voice demands, "then crumple the paper in your hands and toss it into the flames to symbolize the release of your individual mind, embracing your new role in the group."

I stare down at the bold letters, taking a moment to think of what this gesture means.

If you don't like your current story, write a new one.

This is the beginning of my new story.

I take the paper, crumple it between my hands, and toss it into the fire, watching as the paper slowly catches and eventually becomes ash under the fire's blaze.

"Rise," calls a fourth voice, unenthusiastically, "and face your new colleagues."

I rise to my feet, my legs trembling beneath me, and slowly turn to face the source of the voices—four figures, their black-hooded cloaks concealing their identities underneath. In one synchronized motion, the four lift their hands and pull back their hoods, allowing the light of the fire to illuminate their faces.

One of them, a guy with tanned skin and short blond hair, takes a step toward me. His blank expression shifts into a smirk. His teeth are nearly glow-in-the-dark white, and his face is framed with light blond stubble.

"Logan Reeves," he says with an outstretched hand. "Welcome to the Ghost Writers Club."

CHAPTER
SIX
LOGAN

"Jackson Cooper. Nice to meet ya, man"

I take his hand and shake it. His grip is firm as he maintains eye contact. "It's nice to have another guy in the —"

"Hi!" I nearly stumble backward from the abrupt greeting. "I'm Claire."

Before I can even turn to introduce myself, she's already wrapped me in a tight hug, squeezing me like she's been reunited with a friend she has known her entire life. Her voluminous curls tickle my face, filling my nose with the scent of coconut, as I stand with my arms at my sides.

"Okay, give the new guy some space," a familiar voice calls from behind Claire. When she finally lets me go and steps out of the way, I'm met by a face that I recognize.

"Good to see you again, Logan," Julia says, reaching her hand out to me the same way she did the day before.

"Julia," I say, trying to hide the shock in my voice. "But I thought—"

"That I disliked the Ghost Writers? Guess I'm just a good actress." She flicks her shoulder-length brown hair with the back of her hand. "That was just the first part of your test." She gives a wink.

"Test?" I ask.

"To see if you would stick with your instincts and not be easily swayed by outside opinions. I was so happy to see your name come across our inbox. Needless to say, you passed the test." A smile spreads across her face, forming craters in her cheeks. I didn't notice her dimples earlier, but the glow of the fire really accentuates them. I take her hand and give it a shake, allowing my eyes to dart around the library, looking for the source of the fourth voice.

"Did Anna already leave?" Julia asks.

"I think she might have already gone back," Jackson answers, rubbing at the back of his neck.

"Ugh. So lame. Anna hates these sorts of things," Claire chimes in, grabbing hold of my right hand. "Come on! I'll show you to the back room."

She turns and starts toward the door opposite of the fireplace, pulling me behind her like a dog on a leash.

"Claire. Let's maybe not try and scare our newest recruit off on the first day," Jackson says, crossing his arms, a smug grin forming on his face. Claire pauses, looking to me for confirmation. I try to fix my expression so she doesn't see how overwhelmed I feel, but I'm not fast enough. She lets go of my hand, and her face wilts as she drops her gaze to the floor.

"Sorry, Logan. I just get really excited sometimes. We haven't had a new member join since I've been in the group, and I just wanted to—"

"It's fine, Claire," I interrupt. "I'm excited too."

Her face rises, and that bubbly smile returns before she

starts back toward the door. I follow, and Julia and Jackson make their way behind me.

The "Ghost Writer Headquarters," as stated by the plain piece of paper stuck to the side door with a piece of tape, is not what I expected. It's more of a repurposed storage closet. TV carts, boxes, cleaning supplies, and old electronic equipment have been shoved against the walls, forming a sort of barrier around the room. In the middle is a long, rectangular table with six office chairs surrounding it, covered in various bags, coffee cups, open laptops, and notebooks in an array of colors and styles. In the back corner is a clothing rack, where the fourth member of the group has already removed her cloak and hung it from one of the empty wire hangers. She's typing vigorously on her phone, her nails clicking against the screen, refusing to acknowledge anyone as we enter the room.

"Anna. Don't you want to meet our newest recruit?" Claire says, nudging her to look up from her device.

"Hey. I'm Anna." Her voice is monotone as she continues to type.

"Come on, babe, put the phone down for a sec and—"

"Jackson." Her voice is more pointed now. "Please be sure to keep things professional in front of the new recruit. We've talked about this." She flicks her cold gaze to Jackson before landing it on me. My body tenses, like she has me trapped in a block of ice, and I can't seem to move. She lowers her phone and places it on the table by the laptop. I notice it has a House Slytherin sticker pasted on the back. As she makes her way toward me, her high heels clack against the cement floor, and the long black hair that cascades down her back swishes from side to side.

"Sorry. Work never stops, even for the new kid. Nice to meet you, Logan."

I reach my hand out to her as a formality, but she doesn't take it.

"Sorry, I would shake your hand, but I just got my nails done, and I don't want to mess them up." She raises a hand to wiggle her manicured fingers, showing off the deep shade of red covering her nails. "Shall we take our seats?"

Anna gestures toward the table as everyone else finishes hanging their robes on the rack.

I wait a moment, allowing the rest to take their seats until there are only two chairs left. I head for the chair at the head of the table and begin to take my seat.

"Oh. Not there," Julia says, raising a hand and gesturing to the other empty chair.

Is someone else going to be making an appearance tonight?

It's very likely that they would have recruited more than just me, but there was only one seat in front of the fireplace. I do as I'm told and move to the other available chair, letting myself sink slowly until I'm seated. I'm not sure who I should look at, so I let my eyes continue to wander around the room. I look at the TV cart that sits on four wheels in the corner by the long black robes. It's been turned into a makeshift shelf filled with aesthetic stationary and a few fake flowers. On the top shelf is a picture frame, and I squint as I try to make out the image. I give up after a few seconds and turn to Claire, who's staring back at me. I watch as she tracks my line of sight and jumps from her chair, skipping over to the bookshelf.

"Well, I guess before we get down to business, we should give you a little history lesson." She grabs the picture frame from the top shelf.

"Ugh. Is that really necessary?" Anna grumbles, rolling her dark eyes.

"Uh. Duh! If Logan is in the group now, he should know how the group started." Claire moves back to her seat. "Don't you think so, Jackson?"

Jackson's eyes go wide, his gaze bouncing between Claire and Anna as his face turns a bright shade of red. He swallows hard, his Adam's apple bobbing in his wide neck. I look at Anna, who's staring Jackson down with laser focus.

"How about we let Logan decide?" Julia chimes in.

My body goes rigid as all of the eyes in the room turn to me. I feel as though I've looked into the eyes of Medusa herself and my entire body has turned to stone. On one side, I would love to know how the club started. Maybe then I could get a better idea about the girl whose memorial I watched just a few days ago. On the other hand, Anna seems like the kind of person you don't want to piss off.

"Oh for fuck's sake. Claire, just give him the history lesson," Anna says, flicking her hand in Claire's direction before grabbing her phone and returning to her typing.

Claire does a celebratory jump, moving her hands in a clapping motion before taking her seat at the table. Once seated, she slides the picture frame across to me, and I pick it up to inspect it. Five people are crammed in a booth that looks like it was made for only two. The setting in the backdrop looks so familiar, but I can't seem to put my finger on where I know it from.

I recognize each face. Four of them are currently seated at the table with me, and the fifth I saw on a poster from my dorm room window.

"This was taken two years ago, right after our very first

induction ceremony. Jackson, Anna, and Lexi were the founders of the Ghost Writers, and Julia was inducted with me!" Claire says from behind me, pointing to all of the faces in the photo like I haven't just met nearly everyone in it.

Julia's hair is longer in the picture, and she's wearing a flowery sundress like the one I met her in, but this one is covered in roses instead of sunflowers. Jackson has clearly spent some time in the gym since this picture was taken. He has braces in the picture, which explains his perfect teeth, and his frame is so frail and lanky. Claire has braids tied into a ponytail that trails over the front of her shoulders, framing the soccer jersey with the number 43 plastered to her chest. Anna looks the exact same. The only difference I can see from then to now is the look of joy on her face. She looks like she might have been laughing when the picture was taken.

Maybe she and Lexi were close, and when she lost her friend, she was never the same. I can relate. Death takes so much more than the people we love away from us.

"Omg, I would kill for another one of those malt chocolate shakes!" Claire says, pointing to the half-finished shakes that clutter the table. "Rosie's always had the best shakes in town."

Suddenly, a light bulb goes off in my head, and I know exactly where this picture was taken.

"Rosie's Diner?" I ask looking up from the picture.

"Yes!" Claire nearly shouts in my ear, causing me to flinch, but she doesn't seem to notice. "Have you ever been, Logan?"

I nod, looking back at the picture and taking in the black-and-white checkered floor, the ruby-red booths, and the portraits of notable patrons lining the back wall.

"My family would come and visit the campus a lot. They actually met here at Westview."

"Stop," Claire interjects, lightly tapping my shoulder with her hand. "That is too cute. I could cry."

"Can we wait until the end of Logan's story to make commentary? I really don't want to be here all night," Anna says sharply. When my eyes meet hers, she gives me a nod. "Now. You were saying?"

"So. Yeah. My parents would bring me here when my dad was asked to speak for graduations and whatnot, and we made it a tradition to stop by Rosie's before we headed home. Best chocolate malt shake I've ever had."

"If I close my eyes, I can almost taste the chocolatey goodness," Jackson says. "It sucks that they shut it down. They were never able to fully bounce back after 2020."

"Yeah," I say, followed by a long sigh. "We found out when we came to town for move-in day."

I had hoped that my first meal back at Westview would be a Rosie's double deluxe burger and an order of their shoestring fries. My mouth nearly fell to the floor of the car as the diner came into view and I gawked at the state of the place I remembered so fondly. The windows were shattered and boarded up from the inside. Layers of dirt and grime gave the outside of the building a dull hue, like a corpse abandoned by its soul.

I looked over to my mom, who was taking in the dilapidated state of Rosie's. For a moment, she said nothing. I noticed a single tear trickling down her face, catching on her chin, refusing to fall.

"If your dad were here, he would have done everything in his power to save that place," my mom said, her voice a near whisper.

I didn't know what to say then, but in hindsight, I

didn't need to say anything at all. She was right. If my dad were still alive, he would have spent his last dollar keeping Rosie's afloat, but unfortunately, that isn't a reality I have the privilege of living in.

"Man, that's tough," Jackson says, pulling me back to the cluttered room the group calls their headquarters.

"Well this has been lovely," Anna says, standing from the table and packing her things into her oversized bag, "but it's about time we call this meeting to a close. Busy day tomorrow."

Before anyone can protest, she throws her bag over her shoulder and heads for the door. We sit in silence as the sound of her heels echoes throughout the main library until she's gone.

"Sorry about her, Logan," Jackson says. "She has a tough exterior, but once you get to know her, she's not so bad."

"Not so bad?" Claire says, whipping her head toward Jackson. "Just because she's your girlfriend doesn't mean you have to support her when she's being a bitch."

"Claire, please. Not right now." Jackson rises from his chair.

Claire holds his gaze for a few seconds until she finally folds, crossing her arms and letting out a huff. She reaches down and takes the frame from the table in front of me and places it back on the TV cart in the corner. Julia stands from the table, and I follow suit as everyone packs up their things. I don't have anything to pack, but I feel like it would be rude not to wait and walk out with the group.

The air outside seems to only have gotten colder. It whips against my face. I watch as Jackson shuts the large doors and they latch with a loud *click*. He reaches into his bag and pulls out the metal chain that hung from the doors this afternoon, carefully wrapping it through the metal handles and fastening the lock in place.

I'm assuming Jackson has a key, since he was the one with the chain in his bag. But why does he have a key? Who gave it to him?

I want to ask, but I can feel myself starting to fade. I yawn, stretching my arms to the sky, exposing my lower stomach to the chilly air. I quickly lower my arms as Jackson turns to me, reaching out his hand.

"It was great to meet you, Logan. Looking forward to working with you this year. Claire, you still need a ride home?"

"Yes, please! So happy to have you in the group, Logan!" Claire starts before frantically following Jackson in the opposite direction. "We are going to be the best of friends. I just know it!" She gives a wave before turning to catch up to him.

"I promise," Julia starts, "our meetings aren't all like this. Some of us have just had a hard go of it since Lexi passed, and we're all coping the best we can." She places her hand gently on my shoulder before heading after the others. I look past her, but the two of them seem to have evaporated into the night.

———

I kick my shoes off and place them by the door of my dorm room. The floor is cold through my socks, and as I walk to the small thermostat on the wall—sixty-five degrees—I wish more than anything that I could control the temperature in my room. Hopefully this time next year I can be in an apartment of my own.

I throw my phone onto the bed before changing into a

pair of blue sweatpants and a white T-shirt, then sliding my feet into a pair of gray house shoes my mom bought and left on the floor of my closet. I've never worn house shoes a day in my life, and I reiterated to her that I didn't need them. In this moment, I'm glad she didn't listen to me.

After brushing my teeth and placing my toothbrush back in its holder, I'm about to start washing my face when I hear my phone chime from the other room. I shuffle out of the bathroom and make my way over to the bed, where my phone screen is still shining, revealing that I have an unread text message.

Who would be texting me so late at night?

My first thought is that it's from one of the other Ghost Writers, but then a chill runs through my entire body when I realize I never gave any of them my phone number.

I tap on the notification, and my eyes go wide at the words on the screen.

Your new friends aren't who they say they are.

Watch your back or you'll end up like Lexi Pruitt.

Talk soon ;)

—User125249

CHAPTER
SEVEN
LOGAN

The second week of classes has been exactly what you would expect—homework, papers, and *a lot* of caffeine. It's only been a week since I completed my initiation to join the Ghost Writers Club, and the following days have seemed to stretch on endlessly. As Professor Alexander drones on and on, the message I received that night has tugged at my thoughts, relentless.

Clearly, there is someone out there who believes that Lexi was murdered, but *who*? It could be someone in the group, but the way they talked about Lexi the night of my induction, I find it hard to believe that any of them would joke about such a thing. Then again, you can only learn so much about four people in less than an hour.

On the other hand, this could very much be a legitimate warning. If one of them, or all of them for that matter, had a part in ending Lexi's life, I could potentially be their next victim. I pull out my phone and stare at the message as the wheels in my mind begin to turn.

Who would go out of their way to try and protect me?

The only person who comes to mind is my mother, but she has a hard enough time navigating her smartphone. There's no way she would know how to send a text from a blocked number. I flip my phone face down on my desk, closing my eyes in hopes that the answers to all of my questions will fall into my lap.

———

The next meeting of the Ghost Writers is set to take place tonight at eight o'clock, which means that I am mere hours away from walking into a room with a potential murderer —or murderers.

I need to find a killer, and I now have four potential candidates to choose from. The only problem is being able to figure out which one, if any of them, it might be. The tricky part will be to sniff them out while remaining undetected.

I think back to the message from last night. The last line —*talk to you soon*. They made it very clear that this will not be the last time I'll be hearing from them. They also made it very clear that the Ghost Writers are not to be trusted, and if they know more than they're letting on, I hope they plan to share it with me soon.

I make the final decision to keep the text to myself. If any of my new "friends" *did* kill Lexi, I don't want them to know that I know anything. If I find out that it was just a stupid prank, then I can delete the messages and we can all move on with our lives.

The bell rings, its tinny sound signaling that my last class of the day is over. I pack up my things and head back to my dorm to prepare for tonight's meeting, where my investigation into the Ghost Writers will officially begin.

"OMG did you guys hear about Professor Voss?" Claire says excitedly from her place at the table. One look at all of our faces tells her that we have no idea what she's talking about, and she continues. "I heard through the grapevine that he's been siphoning money from his professional account to use on self-care."

"No one is going to want to read a story about a teacher using the school's money to buy face masks," Anna scoffs without looking up from the laptop on the table in front of her.

"He isn't using the money for skin care, though!" Claire responds with the slightest twinge of defensiveness in her voice.

"Okay . . ." Jackson starts, his curiosity getting the better of him. "What was he spending the money on?"

"Massages," Claire says in a hushed tone, like a child saying a word they shouldn't.

"Massages?" Anna echoes, clearly unimpressed. "So what? He's using the school's money to help relieve the stress that working at this school causes him. I would write that off as a professional expense too."

"Okay . . . but what if he was using that money to receive *extra* services?" Claire says as she starts rummaging through her bag.

"Extra services?" Julia asks, raising an eyebrow.

"I'm so glad you asked, Julia!" Claire pulls a small stack of papers from her bag and distributes them around the table. The room goes quiet as we scan the document. It looks to me like an invoice from a massage parlor, advertising a list of charges. The date in the top right corner tells me that this appointment was last week, and the name in the left corner is indeed Timothy Voss. At the bottom, an account number and a scratchy signature that's barely legible.

"What are we looking at?" I ask, searching for something out of the ordinary.

"If you'll turn your attention to the second charge from the bottom," Claire says, referencing the sheet in her hand, "you'll see a charge for 'Paradise' at the cost of two hundred dollars."

Claire looks around the room, waiting anxiously as we connect the dots. I'm not familiar with the establishment, so I pull my phone from my pocket to bring up their website. I tap on the tab that displays all of the services offered, but I'm pulled from my phone when Jackson jolts upright in his chair.

"Holy shit!" he shouts, trying to stifle a laugh. "Professor Voss got a happy ending?"

Claire doesn't say a word, just nods. A giggle escapes her lips.

"I'm sorry, but what exactly is a happy ending?" Julia asks, looking around the room. She catches my gaze for a moment, and I give her a shrug in response. I know what a happy ending is, but I don't want to be the one to tell her.

"He paid to have his masseuse jerk him off," Anna says. Her eyes lock on to Jackson, silencing him.

"Gross!" Julia says.

"Claire. How did you get this?" I ask, taking a mental note of her sleuthing skills. If anyone knows about what happened to Lexi, it'll be Claire. I think to myself that I should try and bring it up to her in private, but it's too soon to risk looking suspicious by asking too many questions.

"There's a girl on my soccer team who works at the

massage parlor as a receptionist to make some extra side money. She was going through and organizing appointments for the week and recognized Voss's name. She sent a screenshot to our group chat, so I DMed her and got more details from there. We looked back at his past invoices and found that the account number charged changed last year—right when Professor Voss started working here."

"Great, but that doesn't prove that he's using school funds," Anna points out, frustration creeping into her voice. "Maybe he just decided to start using a different account."

"I thought you might say something like that. Which is why I have proof." She distributes another printout around the table. "I told Voss I was having computer issues and asked if I could use his computer to buy the book we needed for class. He agreed but told me to be quick, as his next class would be meeting soon. I pulled up the website, and lucky for me, he was already signed in. I quickly went to his account and took a screenshot of his saved payment methods and went on my way. If you compare the account number listed as 'Westview' on Amazon and compare it to the account number listed on the invoice for the massage—"

"It's the same last digits." Jackson finishes her sentence, shock in his eyes. "Claire, this is good. Like scary good. Remind me to never piss you off."

Claire crosses her slender arms across her chest, her deep skin glowing in the dim light. She turns her attention to Anna, and we all follow suit, watching her as she looks back and forth between the two pieces of paper.

"This is a good start. Can you draft this up and have it ready in a week?" Anna finally says, her face remaining emotionless. I turn to Claire, who stands dumbfounded by the words.

"R-really? Yes!" Claire exclaims. "Of course. It will be ready next week!" She takes her seat, an accomplished grin glued to her face.

"Well we have our first story of the year," Anna says. "Please be sure to keep this to yourselves until we are able to publish it next week. Remember, we don't publish old news."

Anna's laptop dings with a notification, and she lowers her eyes to the screen. Her brows knit as she reads the words there.

"Is everything okay?" I ask.

"Check your emails," Anna demands with no further explanation.

The rest of us do as we are told, and I open my inbox to see a message from an unknown sender.

Great. It hasn't even been one full week, and I'm already getting creepy emails from fans of my dad. I was hoping that I could last a semester before needing a new email ID, but the people of the internet surpass my expectations every day. With a click, the email fills my screen. My breath hitches when I see who it's from.

Hello Ghost Writers and congrats on your newest recruit.

Just checking, have you all informed Logan about what really happened to Lexi?

No?

You know, it's only a matter of time until he finds out the kind of people you all really are.

Lexi didn't kill herself, and one of you knows the truth, and until you decide to come clean I will make it my mission to ruin every single one of your lives— one by one.

Don't worry about scaring Logan off. He has his own demons in the closet to atone for.

The way I see it, you all have two options: Find out what happened to Lexi and bring her killer to justice, or do nothing and watch as your worlds crumble around you.

The choice is yours.

Why don't I get us started with a little something I wrote about your very own Jackson Cooper? Just a taste of what's to come if you don't cooperate.

Enjoy :)

CHAPTER
EIGHT

Did you know The International Center of Academic Integrity reports:

- 65 to 75 percent of undergrads admit to cheating at least once.

- 19 to 20 percent of undergrads admit to cheating at least five times.

- 62 percent of undergrads admit to cheating on written assignments at least once.

This got me thinking about what those percentages would be if they were able to include the undergrads who didn't ever admit to cheating. What about the ones that got away with it unscathed? Well, why think about it when you can just ask Jackson Cooper?

To his teachers, Jackson is a star student who is going places, and to his family, he is Mommy and Daddy's future politician. While Jackson Cooper may one day go on to be an elected official, I would think twice before casting your vote for a dirty, filthy cheater.

You see, I found a copy of Jackson's paper that he submitted to Harvard Law, though I'm not sure one could really call it *Jackson's* paper as you'll find many counts of plagiarism weaved throughout. Yes, Jackson Cooper took the time to take a slew of articles on the internet and weave them together to create his own franken-paper, and there is not one original idea to be found on the page.

Honestly, I can't fully blame him, as I'm sure he felt like he had no other choice. You see, it must be hard to create your own ideas when your parents have paid for them your entire life. I guess when Mommy and Daddy are footing the bill, the stakes aren't as high for you.

I'd be interested to see what other works Jackson has carelessly slapped his own name on. Has everything been a lie? Did he even write his own submission to get into the illustrious Ghost Writers Club?

All these answers and more will be revealed until Lexi Pruitt's murderer comes forth. :)

Yours Sincerely,

User125249

CHAPTER
NINE
JACKSON

I read over the article, each word cutting deeper than the one that came before it. Playing sports most of my life, I have undergone my fair share of physical pain, but this hurts worse than any of that.

Yes, it's true that I did the things stated, but I did them for good reason. I want to speak up quickly and defend my actions, but I fear they will fall on deaf ears.

I couldn't care less what the world thinks of me when they read these words. What I *do* care about is what Anna will think. My eyes flit in her direction, and I try to read her expression. Her eyes remain fixed on her screen, but I can tell by the faint redness rushing to her cheeks that she's upset. Angry, sad, or disappointed—I can't tell. Since the accident, Anna has been harder to read. She went off last summer and came back a distant, colder version of herself. I hoped we could work through it, but now that she knows what I've done, I fear I may have lost her forever.

———

I never wanted to be a lawyer.

Not that anyone in my life has ever asked me what I wanted. From a young age, everything was chosen for me.

The clothes I wore to school.

My haircut.

My *girlfriend*.

A couple years ago, when my parents found out that Mayor Flores was going to be running for governor, they saw their opportunity to form a friendship. Actually, I doubt my parents actually have friendships. I would call them partnerships, because it always boils down to what is in it for them. They donated a large sum of money to his campaign in exchange for having a voice in his public policies. They don't care about solving the real issues plaguing the community, so long as they and their precious money are protected.

I guess one good thing did come of this partnership, though—Anna.

With our parents spending so much time together, she and I got close pretty fast. We didn't have a lot in common, but our shared dislike of our lives being molded for us was the kindling needed for our budding friendship. Together, we found our rebellious side. We would sneak out of press meetings and just drive around blaring music, not caring who saw or heard us. We would sneak over to the diner and grab a chocolate malt shake that didn't fit our strict eating restrictions.

"You have to look the part to play the part," we would say mockingly between each sweet sip.

Our favorite thing to do was to go to the train tracks on the outskirts of town. We would lie on the tracks and count the stars together and talk about what life would be like if we could just pick one of the stars and make it our own little island, away from the world.

I never realized how beautiful her eyes were until I saw them filled with hope for a different life. The stars and the moon were full of endless possibilities, and during one of her ramblings about the logistics of building a community on a star, she looked over and caught me staring at her. I looked away quickly, hoping she wouldn't think I was being weird.

"You can kiss me if you want."

Her words caught me off guard. I sat up from the ground, feeling the small rocks shifting beneath me, and Anna did the same. We stared at each other for a moment before I leaned in, letting my lips press against hers, and the stars that filled the sky seemed to shine just a little bit brighter.

On our third trip to the tracks, we consummated our relationship in the back of my SUV with nothing but the moon as a witness to the love we shared.

When you've spent so long in the public eye, you come to learn that everything is done with a purpose. They had deprived us of forming our own relationships in life and done everything to make sure that this one was formed with what we thought was free will. We thought we were being sneaky, but our parents noticed our absence in those press meetings. They knew we were forming a relation- ship, and they were just going to let biology handle the rest. They were setting us up to be the great merger between our families. It was the sense of rebellion that made us fall in love with each other, and once we realized their true intentions, it was ripped away, taking a piece of us with it.

We became the product of money and power coming together. Our relationship would become the symbol to the public that this merging of families wasn't solely formed over whispers and a handshake. We were star-crossed lovers destined to take over the family businesses as well-loved and wealthy political figures.

I still love Anna, and despite finding out we had been pawns in our parents' game, she assured me that her feelings for me remained the same. That she still loved me and she wasn't going to let her parents ruin the one thing in her life that made her happy. This was obviously a relief to hear, and I believed her. But as time went on, she grew more and more distant, and nothing I did could stop the space between us from growing wider.

It started with my surprise birthday party two years ago. The Ghost Writers put together a whole thing at Julia's house to celebrate. I was so happy to spend some time with my friends and doing something that didn't involve writing. It would have been the perfect night—except for the fact that Anna never showed up.

She messaged in the group chat that she wasn't feeling well, but when I texted her in a private chat to make sure she was okay, there wasn't a response. I did my best to enjoy the night without showing how hurt I really was. Over the next couple of days, I reached out occasionally, only to be met with radio silence. After a full week had passed, I stopped by her house, which was just a few doors down from mine, and knocked on the door. Anna's mother answered, and the look on her face told me she was surprised to see me there.

"Oh! Hi Jackson," she said, her eyes bouncing between me and the ornate staircase behind her. "What can I do for you?"

"I was just coming to check on Anna. She hasn't responded to any of my messages, and I was worried about her."

"Sorry, Jackson," she started, "Anna hasn't been feeling well this week and to top it all off, her phone broke and we've just been so busy preparing for the big gala tomorrow that we haven't had time to get her a new one."

"Can I come in?" I asked, trying to look into the house behind her. She shifted slightly, pulling the door to narrow my field of view.

"Anna!" I called into the house behind Mrs. Flores, but there was no sign of her.

"I'll be sure to let her know that you stopped by," Mrs. Flores said with a phony smile, before taking a step back to close the door. I knew that smile. My parents had introduced me to many politicians, and they all had the same soulless smile. If I'd been anyone else, I would have thought she was being genuine, but the many smiles my parents had lied through had taught me to trust no one—not even family.

I stood on the doorstep for a moment, contemplating whether or not to walk around the side of the house to throw rocks at her window like they do in the movies. Something didn't feel right, and I wanted answers, but I knew that I would get a chance to talk to her at the Gala that evening. I couldn't have been more wrong.

When I saw her at the event, we only managed to share a few words before she left so fast that I found myself leaving with more questions than answers.

I hoped that one day I would wake up and find that the Anna I fell in love with had come back to me, but it never happened. I often find myself analyzing everything that I said or did around that time in an attempt to pinpoint the moment things changed between us. Maybe one day she will open up to me, but until then, all I can do is hope.

Now, I look at my phone in disbelief. Yes, I plagiarized my application essay to Harvard Law, but I couldn't let myself do one more thing to follow this path that I felt didn't belong to me. My parents made it very clear that any financial support I received from them was contingent on staying on *their* path, and I was lucky enough to convince them to allow me to do my undergrad here at Westview. They didn't take to the idea immediately, but when I reminded them how close I would be, they gave in. They have always been enticed with the idea of keeping me under their thumb, a mere pawn in their game.

My true passion is writing. It always has been, and as I'm in the last year of my degree, my hope is to land a job working for a publishing company far away from here. I won't need my parents' money to support me.

I can finally start living my own life.

Sure, a small part of me worries what life will be like without their help, but a much larger part of me doesn't care. What I do care about, however, is whether or not Anna will be with me once I make it to the other side. Losing her is what scares me the most.

We have spent so long keeping this facade together, and she is going to kill me if I let something as stupid as a plagiarized paper be the stone that sends our house of cards tumbling to the ground. If this article gets out, my parents will no longer fund my education, I will be forced to withdraw, and my plan for a new life will be over before it can even start. I have to keep this from getting out—not for my sake, but for Anna's.

I read through the first part of the message again, too

afraid to lift my eyes and meet the judging stares that await me.

Does this person really believe that one of us could have killed Lexi? Yeah, she might have ruffled some feathers, but that's just who she was. If she felt strongly enough about something, she would use her very last breath to get the final word in. This made her a great writer, and when you read one of her pieces, you could almost feel her passion jumping off the page.

In the middle of our sophomore year, Lexi and I met up for a coffee after class like we had done many times before. During these meetings of the minds, we would talk about life, share conspiracy theories, and work on whatever article we were in charge of. It was during one of these writing sessions that Lexi said something I'll never forget.

"Since the beginning of humanity, people have searched for something to believe in—a higher power, the universe, the stars, nature. Once you find that thing you believe in so passionately and use words in just the right way, people will abandon ship and be eating out of the palm of your hand."

Lexi said a lot of things. Most of the time, she was just heated, and we let her ride the wave of whatever tangent she felt strongly about that day, but this one caught me off guard. I have seen it happen first hand; Anna and I were the product of what money and power can do to a person. I promised myself and Anna that no matter where we ended up, I would never let myself resort to the things I'd seen our parents doing behind closed doors.

This group isn't perfect, but I can't let myself believe that one of us could have had a hand in ending Lexi's life. Lexi always had a fire that seemed to rage endlessly within her.

If someone in this room was capable of dousing that flame once and for all, who knows what else they're capable of? I need to keep Anna safe, but who knows if she will even talk to me now that she knows what I have done? She has always been the more motivated one between the two of us. I will do everything to make sure she escapes, even if that means I don't make it out of Westview alive.

CHAPTER
TEN
LOGAN

Jackson looks up from his phone, scanning each of our faces before landing on Anna's icy glare. He takes a deep breath, then lowers his eyes in shame. I can't help but feel sorry for him. From what I can tell, their relationship doesn't seem to be in the best place, and if this article is true, I can only imagine what Anna will have to say to him about it.

I glance at her. She seems at a loss for words, her silence like a dagger held against his neck. One wrong move and Jackson will be bleeding out on the floor.

"Anna," he manages to murmur.

"Is this true?" Anna snaps, slamming her phone down on the table.

Jackson doesn't need to respond. The answer is written all over his face. His cheeks have broken out in rose-colored splotches, and he leans forward, placing his face into his hands.

"I'm so sorry, Anna."

"You're sorry?" Her voice rises in volume. "After

everything we've been through. Everything we have worked for." She takes a moment to collect herself before pointing a manicured finger in Jackson's direction. "You may have just single-handedly ruined everything, and you're sorry? Who else knows about this?"

"I didn't tell anyone, I swear."

"Well clearly, you told someone. Otherwise, they wouldn't have written a full fucking article about it."

I feel I should speak up and share the message I received the night of my induction. Whoever this person is has now informed the entire group that Lexi's death was no accident, and if I was correct in assuming that one of the Ghost Writers happens to be a killer, they are now on high alert. I tuck all of this information in the back of my mind and stay silent in my chair.

"Can't you just deny it?" Claire asks cautiously.

"Yeah, I could, but—"

"No." Anna cuts him off. "You *will*. I'm sure my dad can take care of this. Say it was an accident, you submitted the wrong file—I don't know. But we will make this go away."

Jackson sits up as if to protest her request, then quickly retreats to his slouched position.

"It looks like this person only sent it to us," Claire says, her phone lifted up to her face.

I mirror her, tapping the top of my screen to see that the list of recipients includes only those currently seated around this table. Claire copies the text in the article before opening a new webpage on her phone. She pastes the text into an empty box on her screen and clicks the SUBMIT button.

"I can't find it anywhere on the internet either," she

says with a hint of pride, "so if we do what they say, we can stop it from coming out, right?"

"Another great idea, Claire. Let's fix this by playing Sherlock fucking Holmes and hunt down an alleged murderer who killed a girl who obviously killed herself." Anna's words send Claire slouching in her chair, mirroring Jackson.

"Well what if we can prove that she killed herself?" Julia chimes in. "If we clear our names and prove that we didn't have anything to do with her death, then whoever is sending this stuff has nothing on us."

"Except they seem to know our secrets—well, they at least know mine," Jackson says.

"I would rather the world know I plagiarized a paper than have them think I murdered someone," Claire says, her cheery tone slowly returning. "And if we can clear our names, then, well—we at least won't be seen as murderers! It's the lesser of two evils!"

"Can we have the room?" Anna says, more like a demand than a request, her eyes never leaving Jackson. I look to Julia and Claire, who nod sheepishly before grabbing their things and standing from the table. I follow suit and march out without another word.

Once we're outside, Julia takes a seat on the stairs that lead to the entrance, letting out a long sigh.

"Poor Jackson," she says, looking out to the trees that speckle the grove just across the street. Claire shivers as she pulls a pink cardigan from her bag and throws it over her head. I take my place on the step next to Julia. I want to ask questions, but I also want to make sure that it feels natural. This seems like as good a time as any to get some information about Jackson and Anna, so I shoot my shot.

"I know I don't know you all that well just yet, but I don't see how any of you do it."

"Do what?" Julia asks, running her hands over her arms to warm herself.

"Anna," I whisper, as if she will somehow hear me from the back room of the library. "I don't know. She just seems to be kind of—" I pause, choosing my words carefully.

"Bitchy?" Claire says, stifling a laugh.

"Well," I say, trying to hide my amusement, "that isn't exactly the word I would have used."

"Don't feel bad, Logan," Julia says, her focus still on the trees across the street. "We've all thought it once or twice."

"Has she always been this way?" I ask.

A moment of silence follows, sending my thoughts into a swirl of panic. I know I'm asking a lot of questions, but I feel like this is normal for the new kid to ask. Claire and Julia lock eyes, sharing a knowing look. I wish I could read their thoughts and see whatever memory the two of them are calling on. As I wait for their response, I realize just how little I know about these people and the things this group has gone through together. That familiarity would usually come with time, but with this internet stalker on the loose, I'm afraid that time is becoming a limited resource.

"Believe it or not," Julia starts, "there once was a time where Anna was a joy to be around."

"Yeah," Claire chimes in, "she's the one who actually recruited me to join the Ghost Writers. We met at a party when I was a freshman and she was a sophomore. She basically saved me from some asshole senior who was hitting on me. She literally embarrassed him in front of the entire party. It was the coolest thing anyone has ever done for me!"

"Oh yeah," Julia says, her lips stretching into a smile. "What was his name again?"

"Benson." Claire's face twists with disgust. "That guy was the *worst*. Who knows what would have happened if Anna hadn't been there."

I take in their words, trying to match it with the Anna I have come to know over the past week, but I can't imagine Anna sticking up for anyone other than herself.

"So what changed?" I ask, turning to glance at the heavy doors behind me. We remain quiet, listening for any sign of footsteps. Since Anna's shoe of choice always seems to be a high heel, we would hear her coming long before she ever heard us.

"I think it started at the end of freshman year," Julia says, letting her finger comb through her light brown hair. "Anna was a sophomore, and the week of finals, she got sick and had to virtually complete the rest of her assignments. None of us thought anything of it, because according to Jackson, she did the same thing her freshman year. Something about driving to campus each day to take a single test being a waste of her time."

"Okay, " I say, fighting the urge to roll my eyes. "So what was different about the second summer?"

"Well, usually we all keep in touch, but Anna totally went radio silent. Jackson couldn't even get her to respond, and that's saying something. I think he said there was something wrong with her phone or something? I don't know, but it stayed like that for most of the summer. The only time we heard from her was when the news broke about . . ." Claire's voice trails off. "When we held our first meeting the next year, we all just expected her to not show up."

"Did she?" I ask, prompting a scoff from Julia.

"Oh yeah, she did. She always knew how to make an entrance, but when she came in, it was like someone had snatched Anna and traded her for someone who was twenty pounds lighter and wore high heels every day. Before then, Anna wouldn't be caught dead in anything that wasn't a flat."

We sit in silence for a moment, and I take the time to process everything I have learned so far. Anna disappeared for months, and while she was gone, Lexi wound up dead. To top it all off, when she returns to the group, she looks and acts like a completely different person and like she didn't just fall off the face of the earth.

What happened while she was gone all that time? And what does it have to do with Lexi?

I want to ask more questions, specifically ones involving Lexi and how the group feels about what happened. Do they all believe it was a suicide, or do they believe deep down that there was foul play involved?

"So what do we do now?" I ask, burying my hands into my jacket pockets for warmth.

"I don't know," Julia says with a sigh.

"How did the report say that Lexi died?" I ask. "I know they said it was suicide, but did they ever mention how she did it?"

"Well, her mom and stepdad didn't want all of the details released to the public, which is kind of annoying," Claire starts, "but I heard through the grapevine that she overdosed."

"Oh God," I say, a chill working its way down my spine. "That's horrible."

A stabbing pain rises in my chest, like salt being poured over an old wound. Sure, I had friends growing up, but Caroline and Emily truly felt like the siblings I never had. I met them in middle school, and from that day on, we were inseparable. We would spend every waking hour we could together. It got to the point where Emily's mom would say that we were long-lost siblings, and eventually we started to refer to each other as brother and sister.

We started our own little book club together, where we would take turns choosing a book. Emily and I would typically reach for the mystery/thriller books, while Caroline almost always wanted to read a cozy romance. Romance isn't typically my cup of tea, but I would find myself really rooting for the couple to get together by the end. There was something about those stories that was like chicken soup for the soul. I never told any of them this, but when we read *They Both Die at the End* by Adam Silvera, I cried myself to sleep that night. It was such a haunting story, and to this day, if I think about it too much, tears start to gather under my eyes, especially now that Caroline is no longer here.

I was over at Emily's house helping her set up our usual book fort, fashioned from couch cushions and blankets. Caroline was running late, which was typical for her, but it was usually accompanied by an apologetic text telling us that she would be there soon.

We had finished setting up the fort and checked our phones to find that there was no text from Caroline. We both ran over to the window that conveniently provided a great view of Caroline's house. Usually by now, we would see her fast-walking down the street, her auburn hair tied into a tight ponytail. Instead, we were greeted by the flashing lights of an ambulance.

I remember the way my heart dropped into the pit of my stomach. Something was wrong, but at the time, I didn't know what it was. The sound of footsteps approaching the door to the upstairs loft tugged our attention from the window, and we turned to see Emily's mom standing there silently, her eyes red and her face streaked with tears.

"Mom," Emily said, swallowing the lump in her throat. "What's wrong?"

I stood there next to her for what felt like an eternity, waiting for her mom to speak. The longer she stood silent, the more my body filled with the feeling of dread. She closed her eyes and took in a shaky breath before she finally spoke.

"It's Caroline."

"What happened?" Emily said, stepping toward her mother. "Did she get hurt?"

She just stared at us. Looking back, I know she was terrified to tell us that our best friend had taken her own life. It couldn't have been easy for her to share information she knew would shatter us. Parents try so hard to protect their child from pain, but there is no protection against death. No shield to dull the hurt.

I had never seen Emily so upset. I stood in shock as she kicked and clawed at the fort we had built until it was nothing more than a pile of pillows and blankets. Seeing the product of her destruction, she crumpled to the floor and cried. I approached her with caution and took my place next to her and we lay on the soft pile until we both felt dehydrated from crying.

We never built another fort after that night. It felt like it was always our thing, and without Caroline, there would always be something missing. Emily and I still hung out, but it was never the same, and when she went off to college two states away, we saw each other even less.

When I was in the hospital after my accident, I was happy to hear she came and visited me. I was asleep when she stopped by, but when I woke up from one of my drug-induced comas, there were flowers and a stack of three books she had left for me to read during my recovery—two mystery/thrillers and a romance.

We might not talk as much, but I think of Emily—and Caroline—often and try to hold on to the joy we shared with each other before it was stripped away in the blink of an eye. I have never been able to wrap my mind around why Caroline took her own life. She always seemed so happy around me and Emily, but they say it's the ones who smile often who carry the most hurt.

I wonder if it was the same for Lexi. Were there signs that she had been feeling this way, or were the Ghost Writers as blindsided as I was? I know how losing Caroline affected me, and I can only assume that the abrupt loss of Lexi did the same to those who called her a friend.

"Do you guys know what she took?" I ask, a slight break in my voice.

"There was speculation," Julia says. "Some claimed it was painkillers, others assumed it was some other hardcore drug, but as far as I know, Lexi never did anything more than smoke weed on occasion. She said it helped her sleep."

"Well, you can't overdose on weed, can you?" Claire asks rhetorically. "So it has to have been something else." She stands silently for a few seconds, swaying back and forth. Then a light bulb goes off, and her face bursts into a smile. "Oh, I know! We can maybe pull her file at the pharmacy and see if she got anything specific around the time before she . . ." Her words trail off.

"Isn't that like a breach of confidentiality or something?" Julia asks, leaning back on her hands.

"I mean, technically yes. But no one is going to know. We'll be in and out in no time!"

"We?" I ask, sitting upright.

"Yeah!" Claire shouts, nearly jumping up and down. "It will be like a top-secret mission. I have a spare key—perks of my family owning the place—so we can't get dinged for breaking and entering. And if someone catches us, I'll just say that I had a migraine and needed to grab some Excedrin. Easy, peasy!"

I look at Julia, and her eyes meet mine. I break our gaze and look to the large double doors behind me. We've been out here for a while. I can only assume that Anna is still laying into Jackson, but the rustling leaves and singing bugs make it impossible to hear anything on the other side of the doors.

"Oh, they'll be in there for a while," Julia says.

"Yeah, you can basically consider this meeting a wash. There's no way either of them are going to want to sit and work after—" Claire stops, her face shifting to worry. "Do you think whoever this person is knows stuff about all of us?"

The thought sends a chill racing down my spine. I haven't been here for long, but a lot of my life can be found on the internet, thanks to my dad. As far as I know, there isn't anything out there about me that could be damning. The only thing I can think of that would be—no. There's no way anyone knows about *that*.

"So?" Claire nudges, crossing her arms over her chest. "Are you guys in? It can just be us, and if we find anything, we can share it with Anna and Jackson at our next meeting."

My eyes fall to the concrete stairs below my feet. While I'm nervous about what we might find, this mission would be useful in uncovering more information to figure out what happened to Lexi. My dad made a living by taking risks, and if I am going to follow in his footsteps, I need to be able to take the same kind.

"I'll do it," I say semi-confidently, looking at Claire, who responds with a toothy grin.

Julia lets out a long sigh but eventually agrees, standing from the steps and throwing her bag over her shoulder. We decide that Claire will pick us up tomorrow night, and if all goes according to plan, we'll make it in and out without anyone ever knowing we were there.

As I walk across campus toward my dorm, I can't help but smile. For so long, I felt like the accident was the end of my life and any sense of normalcy would be stripped from me until my final breath. For a moment, I feel like I am in some sort of dream state and any second I'll wake up and find myself back at home. Trapped. Right now, I feel so free, like I can do anything and go anywhere. I'll admit, looking into Lexi's suicide wasn't on my Westview bingo card, but I don't plan to let this opportunity go to waste. This story will be my contribution to the legacy my dad started, and I plan to uncover the truth—or die trying.

CHAPTER
ELEVEN
LOGAN

The following evening, my phone chimes, letting me know that Claire has pulled into the parking lot on the back side of my building. I'm shuffling through the bottom drawer of my dresser, and my hand lands on a pair of black gloves. If things go south tonight, I want to make sure that nothing can be traced back to me. I shove them deep into my pocket and grab my phone from the bed to send a reply before making my way down to the parking garage.

The closer I get to the ground floor, the more anxious I feel. The unknown of tonight is most likely a factor, but this anxiety is all too familiar. It was months after my accident before I was able to let myself get into a car. When I had to leave the house to go to my first physical therapy session, I nearly had a panic attack in the five minutes it took to drive to the office from my house.

I hoped that as time went on, the feeling would subside, but as it turns out, the psyche doesn't heal as quickly as the body.

I stop at the bottom of the stairs, partly to catch my breath and partly to calm myself before walking out into the night.

Everything is going to be fine. You are fine.

I repeat the words on a loop in my head, hoping that eventually I'll start to believe them. When I make it to the parking lot, I've managed to get my breathing as close to normal as possible. There's a car parked in the loop that snakes its way around the parking lot. As I approach, I can make out Claire, waving excitedly. I look to the passenger seat to find that it's empty. I was hoping Julia would have been the first to be picked up so I could sit in the back, but it doesn't seem as though that will be the case.

Everything is going to be fine.

I repeat the mantra one last time and take a large breath before opening the passenger door. As I lower myself into the car, the sound of crunching underfoot catches my attention. Food wrappers and old fast-food bags cover the passenger-side floor.

"Sorry my car is a mess. Feel free to just step on whatever's down there."

"You've been saying that as long as I've known you," Julia calls from the back seat.

I whip my head around and see her laughing at Claire, who is dramatically pretending to be offended after being called out, and I manage a laugh with them. It makes sense that Julia would choose the back seat over the throne of trash up front. Despite the mess, the car actually smells of coconut, which I'm quite fond of. It reminds me of the trips we would take to the beach every summer as a family. My parents would always let me order a virgin piña colada, which always came topped with whipped cream, a slice of pineapple, and a cherry.

I miss those days, but the happy memory soothes my nerves for a moment. Claire throws the car into drive, and I quickly scramble for the seat belt to fasten it. Claire turns on some music, and Julia pulls her phone from her bag. Once I feel secure and hear the click of the seat belt, I take a deep breath and close my eyes. I'm back on the beach, playing in the sand and helping my dad build a sandcastle while my mom searches for sea shells to decorate the outside.

———

The car comes to a stop, pulling me from my memory.

"Okay! We're here!" Claire says.

She and Julia unbuckle their seat belts and step out onto the street. I turn to look out the passenger window to the pharmacy, a quaint space wedged between two brick buildings on either side. An unlit neon sign mounted above the door spells out *Martin Medicines*, and a dim glow pours through the front-facing windows, lighting the sidewalk below. I unbuckle myself and open the door, stepping out onto the sidewalk as Claire searches her purse for the keys.

"I know they're in here somewhere," she says, shoving her hand around the bottom of her bag.

Julia gives me a nudge. "Claire would lose her head if it wasn't attached."

"No, I wouldn't! They're in here somewhere," Claire snaps back, continuing her search for the keys.

Finally, with a triumphant smile, she pulls out a large ring of keys covered in pink fuzzy bobbles.

"See, I told you they were in here!"

She fondles the keychain until she lands on a bronze

key, placing it into the lock. When she twists it, a deep click sounds from within the door, and she makes her way into the pharmacy. She heads quickly to a number pad on the wall next to the door and presses a series of digits, prompting a monotone beeping sound.

The lights brighten as we head inside. There must be a motion sensor somewhere in here, so I look around the beige walls, stopping when I see a camera mounted in the corner facing the entrance.

"Don't worry. That camera is just for show. It doesn't actually work," Claire says, walking down the middle aisle toward the back counter.

I stare at the camera a little longer. If it doesn't work, then why is there a red light flashing on and off? I feel a tingle go through my body, just like I did on my first day at Westview. I can't help but feel like we're being watched.

"Logan, are you okay?" Julia asks, placing a hand on my shoulder.

"Yeah. Just looking around," I lie.

We make our way down the center aisle of the pharmacy toward Claire. Each aisle is lined with over-the-counter drugs and medical supplies categorized by ailment. As we reach the end of the cold and flu section, I find Claire searching her key ring for the one that matches the door to the back of the pharmacy. *EMPLOYEES ONLY* is plastered in bold red letters across the door. Claire's fingers stop on a small bronze key, and she inserts it, twisting it until the door opens with a push.

"Don't touch anything," Claire demands as we file into the back room. I'm immediately overwhelmed by the shelves of prescriptions and bottles of medicine. This pharmacy has been up and running for longer than I've been alive, so they must be doing something right. I continue to look around at the shelves bursting at the seams with little white paper bags, all labeled and placed in alphabetical order. I find myself going over to the section marked with a *P*. I sift through the shelf, glancing at the names listed on the labels: Prescott, Presley, Progue—Pruitt.

I pull the bag from the shelf and inspect it further. This prescription is for someone named Adelaide Pruitt. The name doesn't ring any bells, so I look at the bottom of the label and see that she was prescribed clonazepam and olanzapine. I recognize the first drug, but the second one is a mystery to me.

When I was able to start getting out of the house again, my mom set me up with a therapist, who prescribed me clonazepam to help me with my anxiety about being in a car after the accident. I hated how drowsy it made me feel. Sure, it helped my anxiety, but only because I was too tired to feel anxious. After a month or two, I decided I would rather deal with my anxiety than be a walking zombie.

I pull out my phone to search for the second drug.

"What are you doing?" Claire says sternly.

My body jolts, and I nearly throw my phone to the ground. Once I manage to recover, I turn to see her at the end of the aisle, her arms crossed over her chest and her face expressionless.

"I— I was just—" I scramble to place the paper bag back on the shelf. "I'm sorry."

I look back to Claire, who's now fighting to suppress a laugh. A smile has replaced the flat expression from before, and she drops her hands to her stomach as the laugh escapes her.

"I'm totally kidding, Logan! You didn't know I was such a good actress, did you?"

I swallow, feeling the adrenaline still coursing through

my veins. I smile back at her and take a few slow breaths to calm my heart, which feels like it's beating right against the bones in my chest.

"Actress is a bit of a stretch there, Claire," Julia says, crossing her arms in imitation before joining in on the laughter.

"D-did you guys find anything?" I manage to say.

"We pulled her file," Julia starts, "but according to her record, she was only being prescribed a mild antidepressant."

"So basically, she was just like every other person who chooses art as a career," Claire says with a shrug. "What about you? Did you find anything good?"

I look back to the bag that I haphazardly placed back onto the shelf, only when I look at it this time, I see a small slip of blue paper the size of a Post-It taped to the backside of the bag. I lift it from the shelf and flip it over to see *Claire* written in black marker.

"I think this is for you," I say, holding the bag out toward Claire, my hands shaking.

She takes it from me, and Julia and I watch as she meticulously removes the note without ripping the bag. Julia and I move in on either side of her as she unfolds the note and we all read it together.

I'm watching you :)

Those three words force the adrenaline back into my body. My heart bounds in my chest as I look through the large plexiglass window to the camera mounted on the wall. The blinking red light only confirms my fear. Is it really possible that whoever this is has been watching us this entire time? The note left for us here tells me that they know where we will be and are one step ahead of us in this investigation. That, or—a shiver slides down my spine at the thought—someone in the group is lying about who they really are.

Suddenly, the sound of a police siren in the distance echoes through the quiet pharmacy, snapping our attention toward the door.

"We need to get out of here," Claire says, breathless. She shoves the note into her pocket and makes a dash for the door that leads back into the pharmacy. Julia and I just stand in shock as the sound of the siren grows closer.

"Now!" Claire shouts. Julia and I snap from our daze and follow her out of the room. Once we're all back in the main area of the pharmacy, she frantically inserts the small bronze key into the door and twists it until the lock clicks back into place.

We dash for the entrance, and with each step we take toward the exit, the sound of the siren becomes more and more clear. They have to be only a street over at this point. Claire drops to a crouch behind the aisle marked *Toiletries*, and we quickly do the same. The three of us peek over the top shelf, watching and waiting. Dread fills me, starting from my feet and lodging itself in my throat. The three of us are so still that I wonder if they can hear my heart racing as well.

A flash of blue fills the pharmacy, sending shadows dancing around the room. My breath hitches. I drop to the floor along with Julia and Claire, awaiting our fate. I'm going over what I would say to the cops in my head when the room goes dark. The siren that signaled the end for us now grows fainter as it drives away.

The three of us stay on the floor, frozen for what feels

like forever. Claire is the first to stand, peeking over the top of the shelf to confirm that the coast is clear. She looks down and meets my eyes before giving a nod. I close my eyes and let out a long sigh, resting my head on my knees.

"That was too close," Julia says, shuffling to her feet. "Now can we please get out of here?"

"Absolutely," Claire says with a shaken voice, offering her hand to me. I take it and start to rise, but then she releases me, sending me back to the ground. I look up and see her now standing with her hand over her chest. She's swaying like she's suddenly intoxicated, and she nearly falls over before Julia puts a hand on her for support.

"Claire, are you okay?" Julia asks.

She takes a few more breaths before finally speaking.

"Yeah, I'm totally fine!" she says as I lift myself from the floor. "Let's get out of here."

Claire heads toward the door, her steps slow and cautious. She looks through the window, checking both ends of the street to make sure there isn't a cop waiting for us. We make our way out onto the street and are almost back to Claire's car when my phone vibrates with another email from our mystery stalker.

CHAPTER
TWELVE

Hello Ghost Writers,

It's me again! I know you have missed me, and boy, have I missed you. I know how much you liked that story about Jackson Cooper, but he was merely the catalyst to this one, and things are about to warm up!

Speaking of warming up, how many of you like to play sports? I've never quite been a fan of them myself, but I have always admired the dedication it takes for someone to perform at such a high level! They are constantly conditioning their bodies with food and exercise to maximize their performance, to be the best athlete they can be.

Genetics also play a big role in how athletic someone can be. Some are born natural athletes, and some are born with hurdles in their way and they will do whatever it takes to claim their prize— even if that means lying.

Yes, I'm talking about you, Claire Martin.

Now, we all know Claire, and many of us even enjoy her company. Her bubbly attitude and bright smile always seem to light up any room that she walks into. A lot of you also know that she is the star of the soccer team here at Westview. The level of athleticism she displays in each of her games is what caught the eye of the United Soccer League.

She has officially submitted all of her documents and has signed all the dotted lines and, if all goes well at her tryouts in a couple months, she will be competing in the USL Championship next year.

Oh, and did I mention that her family owns the pharmacy in town? Very quaint place, with friendly staff. It's so hard these days to find a pharmacy that is family owned what with new chain pharmacies popping up on every street corner in town.

Now, you're probably wondering what this has to do with anything. Well, when your family works in the medical field, you start to have connections with medical professionals. Most of these professionals take their jobs very seriously. They promise to live and die by the regulations in place for them. They take oaths, promising to remain ethical in their pursuit to heal those who need it most. Lucky for Claire, some will do whatever you want them to—that is, if the price is right.

For Claire, this meant showing a little skin to have one of her doctors illegally prescribe her anabolic steroids in order to increase her performance on the field.

She's really gained a following in the last year. Many people have asked her the secret to her success. In an interview highlighting her road to the USL, she claimed that "hard work and persistence" got her to where she is today.

Well Westview, I'm here to inform you that those words were bullshit. In most cases, hard work and persistence is key, but in Claire's case, not so much.

I have to hand it to her, though. She was smart about it. She had the doctor prescribe them under an alias. This way, when she went to the pharmacy after hours to pick up her pills, it wouldn't show up in her file at her family's place of work. Not only would it be a shame if her parents discovered this blatant betrayal of their trust, but it would be a real shame if the USL found out that one of their star candidates was abusing performance-enhancing drugs, now wouldn't it?

Maybe it's time to prescribe the Ghost Writers a dose of the truth.

The truth is always such a hard pill to swallow :)

-User125249

CHAPTER
THIRTEEN
CLAIRE

A single tear falls as I look at the article on my phone.

From a very young age, I wanted to be a professional athlete. Some of my favorite memories with my family were going to soccer games. I would just watch the players running up and down the field, and what stuck out to me the most was they never seemed to grow tired or get out of breath, which is something I could never relate to.

I remember being on the playground in the first grade. Me and the other kids in my class were playing tag, running and screaming, dodging one another to try and be the last person standing. There were only four of us left in the game, and I wanted to be the winner. I was Katniss Everdeen, and I wanted to be the girl on fire. What I didn't know was that my body was going to take me literally.

Someone else was tagged out.

I was in the final three.

Someone else again.

I was now one of two still standing, and I was going to do everything in my power to be the last one.

I think my obsession with winning started when I was a little girl. My grandpa would always yell at the TV when his favorite team lost a game. We had a big party at our house to celebrate our favorite soccer team making it to the first-ever finals of the USL Championship. The dining room table had been transformed into a cornucopia of snacks, dips, drinks, and sweets. The house was decorated in memorabilia, and everyone at the house was dressed in their favorite player's jersey. The night ended with everyone squished into the living room as the game went into overtime. The room was still, and everyone held their breath for what felt like a full five minutes, their eyes fixed on the TV screen. No one made a single sound. Everyone sat at attention, leaning toward the TV as my grandpa paced the floor. Right at the end of overtime, the opposing team scored a game-winning goal and were named the champions of the USL. I remember going up to my grandpa, who was visibly upset, and wrapping my arms around him.

"Don't be sad, Grandpa! They still got a pretty trophy!"

"Silver trophies are for first-place losers," he said, looking down at me with a grimace under his gray-speckled mustache. He leaned down and gave me a fuzzy kiss on my forehead. "If only you had been out on that field, peanut, you might have helped them win that game."

I was only seven when he said those words to me, but it always stuck in the back of my head. Everything I did in life, whether it be a science fair, poetry competition, or soccer game, I wouldn't be satisfied unless I took home the gold. While there were no medals to be handed out in this game of tag, I was still determined to go for gold.

I watched the other two with intense focus. There was one predator. I was one of two prey, and I was determined to make sure that my survival instincts were superior. My feet never stopped moving. The three of us moved cautiously around the field like animals caught in a stand-off, analyzing each other's every move. In a quick jolt, the predator made a mad dash, and his target was me. I quickly shifted and began sprinting in the opposite direction. Each adrenaline-fueled step brought a new gust of wind against my face, throwing my dark, curly locks freely behind me.

Suddenly, I could feel my body forcing me to slow down. Something wasn't right. Every step grew heavier as I struggled to pull air into my lungs. Eventually, the air I was getting wasn't enough, and I fell to the ground, ultimately becoming not only the prey, but the first-place loser. I remember lying on the ground and staring at the sky in defeat as my teacher ran over and shoved my DPI inhaler into my mouth, helping me to sit up. A few slow, medicated inhales later, my breathing returned to normal, and I stood from the ground with nothing more than tightness in my chest and a bruised ego.

That is one of my earliest memories where my asthma kept me from being the winner I knew I could be. Since that day, asthma has plagued every life plan I have ever made for myself, and while it's never completely halted my plans, it has added another layer of challenges to achieve them.

When I got to high school, I did a good deal of research on asthma management for athletes. I found an article where someone sat down and interviewed David

Beckham. I was always a big fan of Beckham, but I became an even bigger fan when I found out that he'd achieved such a successful professional soccer career despite his battle with asthma. That interview became my bible. I did all of the workouts he did. I ate all the same food. I followed everything down to the smallest detail, but it was never enough. My symptoms were alleviated slightly, but not enough to make much of a difference on the field.

With my dreams slowly moving out of reach, my parents thought it would lift my spirits to give me more privileges around the pharmacy. They taught me how to run the register. They let me use my dad's login to learn the system and taught me how to receive and process prescriptions, and I learned the correct way to fill the bottles, and the filing systems that were currently in place. I wasn't allowed to actually fill prescriptions, so most of my time spent at the pharmacy included helping with checks and balances and paying invoices and bills. They slowly gave me everything except the key to the building. My grandfather started Martin Medicines back in the sixties, and he ended up leaving the place to his only son and his wife. My grandfather was so happy the day I was born because he knew one day, another Martin was going to one day inherit the business he'd built from the ground up. My parents had been hinting since the day I turned sixteen that Martin's Medicines would one day be left for me and my future family to take on and continue the legacy.

It felt like my dreams didn't matter to them.

Sure, they knew I had a passion for soccer, but they were never fully sold on the idea of building a career as an athlete. My asthma aside, they would constantly remind me that if I made one wrong move on the field, I could sustain an injury, and it would all be over. Still, they agreed to let me pursue my passion as long as I got my degree.

"It's always good to have a backup plan," my mom would say.

I was going to do everything in my power to make sure that I never had to use that backup plan.

One night, I was lying in my dorm, and I came across another article that analyzed the use of anabolic steroids in asthma patients. In most of the patients, their asthma symptoms were nearly eliminated, but some experienced exacerbated symptoms. After the Beckham method hadn't afforded me the results I was looking for, I was willing to try anything, even if it meant a little lying.

I knew my parents would never go for it.

They were already not sold on my choice of career, and they would never agree to me taking a pill that could potentially lead to irreversibly damaging my body. I knew the risks, but I had to at least try.

By that point, I already had access to a list of doctors who were loyal to the pharmacy. All it took was a reverse search of the drug I wanted to figure out which doctors I should contact. I scrolled down the list until I found a name that rang a bell.

Dr. Anthony J. Huntz.

I'd first learned this doctor's name when I overheard a conversation between two of the girls on the team. One of the girls, Hannah, was bragging to her friend about how she knew this doctor who prescribed her Xanax and Adderall even though she didn't actually need it. All she had to do in return was provide him some "favors," which she never minded because she thought he was hot.

"I would have honestly hooked up with him for nothing, but I would never tell him that," she would say in the locker room.

I had my target.

I've always known I was pretty. I know, that sounds so self-centered of me, but growing up, I have never had an issue attracting the gaze of a man. I never gave them the time of day, though. I had a goal for my life, and the last thing I was going to do was let a man knock me up so he felt as though he had some sort of imaginary power over me.

Women's bodies are powerful and limitless. Men are simple. You give them a little bit of attention and you can pretty much get them to do whatever you want them to do. And I was determined to get what I wanted.

I called and made an appointment for the next day. I walked into the doctor's office in what I would call sporty glam: high-waisted leggings that hugged every curve of my sleek body, a sports bra, and a jacket. I made sure to put moisturizer all over to ensure that any exposed sections of my deep skin caught the lights overhead.

I got into the room with the doctor and explained to him what I wanted to do. I let him think he had all of the power. I maintained eye contact as I played with the already low zipper on my jacket. I moved it up and down and watched as his distracted eyes bounced between mine and my glistening chest. He moved a little closer, and I knew I had him exactly where I wanted him.

I left the office an hour later having achieved my mission. I had him write the prescription under an alias, because I didn't want the steroids to show up in my file at the pharmacy the next time I needed to refill my DPI inhaler. I hoped that after this, I would never need an inhaler again.

The medicine worked. My symptoms were basically gone. I could run farther than I ever had been able to before. I stopped taking them for a few months so that I could pass all of my drug screenings for the USL, but once that was over, I was back on them. I had to go back and see Dr. Huntz until he finally set my prescription up to auto-renew every thirty days.

I had done it.

Staring at my phone now, I can feel every ounce of hope drain from my body, embarrassment filling its place. I look up and see Julia and Logan staring, a twinge of judgment on their faces. I know that face. I've seen it from my parents every time their perfect daughter couldn't meet their standards. I've seen it every time I have tried to tell them that I want to play soccer instead of working in a pharmacy for the rest of my life.

"It's going to be alright, Claire," Julia says, her mouth forming an uncomfortable smile.

But it's too late.

That millisecond of judgment told me all I needed to know.

My mind immediately goes to Anna. What will she think of this? Has she seen it? Of course she's seen it. Even after everything that has happened over the last year—and the way she's treated us—I still care what she thinks of me.

We met at a party when she was a sophomore and I was a freshman. Some guy I didn't know walked right up to me and put his arm on my lower back. Before I could pull away, his arms were wrapped around my body and we were swaying back and forth. Anna saw him move in unannounced, and next thing I knew, the grip around me loosened. I whipped around to see Anna with her drink lifted over his head, letting it slowly pour from the top of his head and stream down his face.

"How 'bout you try fucking someone your own age, Benson," Anna said, loud enough to attract an audience.

Benson scanned the room as it broke out into laughter. He locked eyes with Anna one last time, but never once did she waver. I don't think she even blinked. I was in awe.

Benson broke his gaze and turned away from her, and I watched as he went up the stairs like an animal with its tail tucked between its legs.

"Trust me. You don't want to give Benson a second of your time," Anna said with a nudge. I turned to face her. "Not sure I've seen you around. Are you new here?"

"Yeah. I just started in August. I'm Claire."

"Nice to meet you, Claire. I'm Anna. Sophomore."

"Thanks, Anna, for—" I gesture toward the stairs. "You know, getting rid of—"

"No worries. Benson is the worst. Last year, when I was a freshman, he tried to work his way through our whole class. Stick with me and I'll help you avoid all the Bensons of Westview." Anna looked toward the kitchen and then back to me. "You wanna go grab a drink?"

I looked at my new guardian angel and nodded. She held out her hand, and I took it, and we headed back in to the party.

From that point on, we were pretty much inseparable. That was, until last spring, when Anna grew more and more distant. I understood that she had her own commitments to her family, but even when we would bump into each other on campus, she seemed cold. I remember sitting in class the rest of that day and going over every conversation I'd ever had with her in my head. I couldn't pinpoint any reason she would have to be mad at me, but clearly, I had done something wrong for her to go from being my best friend to not even making eye contact with me as we passed in the hall. I tried to reach out and check on her. The Anna who came to Westview wasn't the same girl who left for summer break. I wanted to make sure she was okay. I found myself checking my phone every other minute, but I never once got a response.

One day, as I was coming out of my last class, I walked through one of the courtyards on campus toward my dorm. I saw Lexi and Anna sitting on one of the benches talking, and as I got closer to them, I realized neither of them were actually talking. Anna was hunched over and sobbing with her face buried into her hands. I started over there, but Lexi's eyes found mine. She didn't say a word, just shook her head in a way that said *Not right now.*

I froze and stood there as her dark eyes bored into mine, willing me to walk by like I never saw them.

The next day, at our Ghost Writers meeting, I waited for Anna or Lexi to pull me aside and let me know what was wrong, but it never happened. Anna was still cold, and Lexi pretended like it had never happened. I didn't want to pry, to make whatever was wrong worse and lose the first friend I had at this school.

I gave her the space in hopes that whatever happened would fix itself and things would go back to the way they were, but it was in vain. I still hold on to what is left of our friendship, and I fear that once she reads this article about me, those last ties will be irreversibly severed.

Now, as I'm standing on the street outside of my family's pharmacy, it feels like my heart has shattered into a million pieces. I want to cry, but it feels like all of the water in my body has dried up. I start to go numb as I feel a tugging in my chest.

Shit. Not now.

I break my stance and head for the driver's-side door of my car. With each step, my breath becomes more laborious, like I'm playing tug-of-war with an invisible force, and air is the rope. My knees buckle out from under me, and I fall to my knees just shy of my car. Logan and Julia quickly spring into action, running toward me.

"What do you need. Where is it?" Logan asks, panic filling his voice.

The lack of air in my lungs prevents words from form-ing, so I point to the front driver's-side door. Logan follows my finger with his eyes and darts toward his target. "Stay with her," he commands Julia.

Logan tears open the door and begins scrabbling around the car. My breath is a wheeze now, and every labored inhale starts to drown out the world around me "Logan! It's getting worse. Have you found it yet?" Julia calls over to the car, tears forming in her eyes.

"I'm trying! I don't see it!" he calls back, his frantic voice rising higher in pitch.

It's in the glove box.

Every part of my body wants to scream.

I try my best to mouth the words to Julia, and she watches every formation of my lips with sheer focus as she sounds out what I can't bring myself to say.

"Guh . . . luh . . . ff . . . bah . . . cks— Glove box!" she says, and I nod. "Logan, it's in the glove box! Hurry!"

A dark circle forms around my vision, closing in with every failed attempt at a breath. I close my eyes and focus on staying alive.

I feel my mouth being forced open, then the cold plastic

against my lips. I lift my hand to find Logan's holding my inhaler to my mouth, and I wrap my fingers around the device, letting my index finger rest on the top. With the last bit of my strength, I press hard on the top and will my lungs to take in air.

Breathe.

My eyes shoot open as the night sky above me comes into focus. I heave myself up into a seated position and cough as the air screams into my lungs. I stay seated with my head resting on my knees until I can regulate my breathing. Logan sits on the sidewalk in front of me, and Julia kneels behind me, rubbing my back. I take in one deep breath, followed by a long sigh.

"Thank you," I manage to squeak out through my burning throat.

Logan and Julia don't say anything back, just sit there in comforting quiet. Coexisting with me, until I am ready to move.

I think about how to move forward from here, not just physically, but emotionally. I worked so hard for my career as a professional athlete, and it's all over for me if this article gets out. I've seen this before. The media doesn't ask questions, and they sure as hell don't care whose life is ruined as long as they can break the story first. My parents will never fully trust me again. My best friend will think terribly of me. I'll have nothing.

Every part of me wants to peel myself from the sidewalk and run as far as I can and never look back.

Unfortunately, in my condition, that isn't very far.

CHAPTER
FOURTEEN
LOGAN

The next morning, I can hardly keep my eyes open. Julia and I waited with Claire until she was okay enough to drive. Julia wanted to call her an ambulance, but Claire insisted that she would be fine, and she just needed a moment to catch her breath.

The whole ride home, she acted as though we hadn't witnessed her almost die in the middle of the street.

"That was crazy, wasn't it?" Claire said with a giggle.

A bit of an understatement, but I nodded with a forced smile.

Back in my dorm, I tossed and turned, building a dam to hold back the thoughts rushing to me from all directions.

It feels as though I've just fallen asleep when my alarm clock chimes at the start of a new day. Through half-opened eyes, I check my phone. I'm about to message Claire to make sure she's okay when I see a message from Anna calling an emergency meeting for tonight.

This can't be good, I think as I rip myself from the

comfort of my bed. In truth, the bed itself isn't all that comfortable, but as tired as I feel, lying down anywhere for the rest of the day would be a luxury.

Each class that passes is a step closer to a meeting I'm not sure I want to attend, but at the end of the day, I have a job to do. I *will* find out what happened to Lexi—and whether or not the Ghost Writers are to blame. I just have to get through a few more meetings, ask my questions, and it will all be over.

———

"I can't believe you would jeopardize your entire athletic career. How could you be so stupid?" Anna seethes, leaning toward Claire with her palms pressing on the table.

"Yeah?" Claire starts, rising slowly from the table, her eyes fixed on Anna's. "Well, since when do you care about anything I do these days?"

"I care because how do you think this will make the rest of us look? If you're abusing steroids, people are going to think we're all druggies like you!"

"I don't even use them anymore, and besides, no one on campus knows who the Ghost Writers are, so your precious name will be safe."

"God. How dense can you be?" Anna says, her words sharp. "If this person releases these articles, the entire campus will know who the Ghost Writers are. They will make assumptions about each and every one of us without a second thought." She pauses, looking around the table. "You all understand that, right?"

"But if we can—" Claire's voice breaks, and she sinks back into her chair. She blinks rapidly, keeping the tears from filling her eyes. "I feel guilty enough about stealing from my parents, okay? And besides, I don't even know how anyone could have found out. I never told anyone, and when I stopped, I didn't think I'd ever have to bring it up."

"Well, you must have brought it up to someone, because how else would someone be able to write about it?"

The room goes silent. So silent that I can hear the electricity humming in the walls. I never noticed it until now. Truthfully, I was expecting to be dismissed like last time, but Anna seems to have no issue berating Claire in front of the entire group. I would rather be shivering on the stairs outside than be here to watch Claire wilt into the floor.

The room itself seems to vibrate as our phones buzz in sync.

Not again.

My mood shifts from pity to fear. I begin to tug on the frayed sleeve of my jacket, too afraid to lift my phone from the table. It hasn't even been a full twenty-four hours, and this person is already trying to add more fuel to the fire.

Anna plops down into her seat with a huff and pulls her phone from her bag. We all watch as she taps the screen, her long red fingernails clacking on the glass.

"Well?" Julia says, her breath shaking.

"Old news." Anna scoffs, rolling her eyes.

Old news? I lift my phone and open the notification, and the rest of the group does the same. When the message finally loads, I see that it's a clipping from an old news story. Upon further inspection, I realize this isn't just any old news story—it's the article that was published after Lexi was found dead.

My eyes go wide as I scan through it, making a mental note of each detail that might be useful.

Lexi left her family home late at night on July 30.

She was found in her car on the side of the road, unconscious behind the wheel.

Her cause of death was deemed to be a combination of drugs in her system, leading to an overdose and the failure of her heart.

She is survived by her mother and stepfather, who have chosen not to speak to the press at this time.

"We already know all of this," Jackson says in a flat tone. "Why would they send us an article we've already seen?"

"Who cares? We have more important things to worry about," Anna says, tossing her long, jet-black hair over her shoulder.

"I don't know," Claire starts. "Maybe they sent this to us for a reason. Like a clue or something!"

"Yeah?" Jackson says, sitting up in his chair, "So you're telling me that whoever this life-ruiner is, they had a sudden change of heart and are now delivering us clues on a silver platter? I doubt it."

"Well, we've all seen this article already," Julia points out. "Is anything jumping out to anyone else? Because I've got nothing."

"Maybe if we look at . . ." Claire's voice trails off as Anna stands from the table, collecting her things and placing them in her bag. "Where are you going?"

"I don't have time for this," Anna says, making her way toward the door. "I have better things to do than to play Sherlock Holmes with a bunch of wannabe detectives."

She leaves the room without another word, the door slamming behind her. Jackson is the first to run after her. I assume he's going to try and get her to come back to the meeting, but I have a feeling we've seen the last of Anna Flores for the night.

"She doesn't deserve him," Claire says through gritted teeth, wiping a tear from her cheek. "She treats him like shit on the bottom of her Louboutin heel, and he just takes it."

"Claire," Julia says, trying to place her hand on Claire's, but she pulls it away before she can make contact. She shoves her chair backward, nearly knocking over the stack of boxes behind her, and storms out of the room. Julia chases after her, and I'm left alone at the table. It's only a few seconds though before Julia walks back in, releasing a sigh and leaning against the door.

"Well, I guess this meeting is over. If you want to head out, I'll text Jackson to come back and lock up the front doors."

"I can wait with you if you want."

"No, it's fine. I want to check in on Jackson anyway. He's had a rough go of things this last year, and I just want to make sure he's okay."

I give her a nod and make my way out of the old library toward my dorm. Campus is quiet at night. A little too quiet. In the movies we used to watch on our family movie nights, they made it seem as though in college there was always some sort of party happening at any given time, but here, it's the exact opposite. I'm not complaining. I've never been the party type myself, and usually if a gathering involves more than ten people, I'd rather just stay home.

I reach the far end of the grove, then turn to look at the library in the distance. In the dim lighting that surrounds it, the building looks like someone took scissors and cut a hole in the middle of a backdrop, leaving an empty black rectangle in its place. Like a dark portal to lands unknown.

When I make it back to my dorm, I throw my bag to the floor and plop onto the twin size bed, staring at the flat white ceiling overhead. I close my eyes and try to silence the thoughts that clang around in my skull, to no avail.

I sit up on the bed and open my phone. The screen is filled with the article covering the night Lexi died. I go over the facts again.

Lexi left her family home late at night on July 30.

She was found in her car on the side of the road, unconscious behind the wheel.

Her cause of death was deemed to be a combination of drugs in her system, leading to an overdose and the failure of her heart.

She is survived by her mother and stepfather, who have chosen not to speak to the press at this time.

There must be some vital detail here that hints at what happened that night. Why else would this mystery person be sending the group something we've all already seen?

Maybe whoever this is knows what I'm really doing here, and they're sending me clues.

The thought sends a chill through me colder than ice. There is no way *anyone* could know, but whoever this is seems to have a knack for uncovering the things people don't want to get out. I push the thought from my head and reach for my laptop where it rests on my nightstand.

When the computer comes to life, I immediately go to the browser at the bottom. I type Lexi's full name into the search bar and press enter. I don't know what I'm looking for, but there must be something on the internet that can provide me with more information than the article currently displayed on my phone. When the search results pull up, I feel my breath hitch in my chest.

I stare at the headline of the top article: *Sean Reynolds, Stepfather of Lexi Pruitt, Reported Missing*.

I scan the screen and see that it was posted only a few short hours ago. I click the link and learn that as of today, Sean Reynolds has been missing for over forty-eight hours. There is a quote from Adelaide Reynolds, his wife I assume, saying that he went to work one day and never came home. I scroll down and see the portrait of an older man with salt-and-pepper hair tousled on top of his head. Deep purple circles sag below his eyes, and he looks as though he hasn't slept in at least a week.

Before I can read further, my phone vibrates against the bed. I lift it to see a text notification from Julia.

Coffee bar. Tomorrow @8AM. We need to talk.

———

The next morning, I yawn as I wait in line for my coffee. I raise my arm to look at my watch—ten till eight. I look around the crowded lobby, searching for Julia's face, but there's no sign of her. No notifications on my phone, either.

When I finally get my coffee, I settle into one of the chairs in the lounge area just in front of the coffee bar. I take a sip and close my eyes as the dark liquid warms me from the inside. I lift my watch and see that it's now five minutes past the time Julia wanted to meet, and I glance back to the line to see if maybe I missed her coming in. When I can't find her by the coffee bar, I look back to the entrance of the building and spot her running in, clearly frantic based on her slightly disheveled hair.

She spots me and makes her way over, plopping down into the chair directly across from me.

"Hi. So sorry I'm late," she says as she attempts to fix her hair.

"Rough morning?" I ask, offering a friendly smile.

"Yes. It turns out when you set your alarm for six in the evening, it doesn't go off at six in the morning."

Once Julia has gotten herself together, she looks around the lounge area before leaning in toward me.

"Did you see it?"

I assume Julia is asking if I saw the article about Lexi's stepdad going missing. I'm glad to know that I wasn't the only one going down a rabbit hole last night. I give her a knowing nod.

"Do you think something bad happened to him?"

Julia pulls her phone out of her bag and taps around on the screen in silence. Once she finds what she's looking for, she lays it on the table in front of me.

"So, I'm assuming you saw this?"

I look at the phone and recognize the same tired, rugged face and the word *MISSING* stretched across the top.

"Yeah. I saw it last night in my dorm room after the meeting. Did you know him?"

Julia's face tightens like she's just been punched in the stomach. "I guess you can say that. We never really inter-acted, but I've been in the same room as him. All I really know about him is stuff that Lexi told me."

"What kind of stuff did she tell you about him?"

"He, um . . ." Julia lowers her eyes and takes a deep breath. "Let's just say he isn't a good person."

"Did he do something to . . ." The words catch in my throat. Julia starts to speak, but she stops before the thought can form, and I have my answer. "So what do you think happened to him?" I say, changing the subject.

"I don't know."

"Okay . . . so what did you want to meet me about?"

Julia takes a moment to look around as though she suspects someone is listening to our conversation. "I have a theory."

"A theory?" I ask with a raised eyebrow.

"Yes. About Sean's disappearance. Lexi has been dead for over a year. Don't you think it's weird that after all this time, her stepdad goes missing right when someone is targeting us about her death?"

"It's definitely a strong coincidence otherwise."

"I don't think it's a coincidence at all. I had my"—Julia pauses and lowers her voice to a whisper—"suspicions of him back when the news about Lexi broke. With my dad being a police officer and my summer job at the station, I had access to all of the information surrounding her death. So, I did my own investigation. I suspected him for a while, but nothing ever led to a concrete answer, ya know? And when the autopsy came back as a suicide, I gave up and left it alone."

"And now that our cyberstalker seems to think that she was murdered . . ."

"Those same thoughts I had over a year ago started to come back up."

"So, what exactly did Lexi tell you he did? Do you think he could have killed her?" I ask before I can stop the words from leaving my mouth.

"He was . . ." Julia pauses, contemplating her words. "He is an alcoholic. A belligerent one at that, and when he would come home after a night of drinking, he would"— she takes in a sharp breath—"hit her."

"Holy shit," I whisper with wide eyes.

Julia's lips tighten to a thin line, and she nods slowly.

"Do you think he's actually missing? Could her stepdad be the one behind all of this?" I ask, but before she can answer, my phone vibrates against the table. Julia's phone chimes a second later, and I immediately get this sinking feeling in the pit of my stomach. I lift the phone to see a message from Anna.

> OLD LIBRARY! NOW! THERE'S BEEN A BREAK-IN!

Julia is already on her feet, slinging her bag over her shoulders. I quickly follow suit, and we rush over to the Old Library.

The whole way, Julia and I don't say a word, which I appreciate since all of my oxygen is being used to keep up with her. It's been a while since I've had to walk this far at such a fast pace, but I take all of the pain I feel in my body and shove it to the back of my mind.

When we finally arrive at our destination, the first thing that I notice is the chain, now lying on the ground, broken into two pieces. We approach the front door, which stands ajar, and when I bend down to inspect the chain, I realize that it isn't broken—it's been cut.

I know that the obvious answer would be to assume that our internet stalker is the culprit, but then again, bolt cutters aren't hard to come by. It could have been a home-less person looking to get out of the cold night air.

God. Please let it just be a homeless person.

I stand from the ground, feeling the ache that has now settled between my bones, and follow Julia into the dark. As we make our way to the back of the long hallway, I focus on keeping my breath calm and steady. I'm still attempting to catch my breath from our rush over here, but also, I don't want whoever might be lurking in here with us to hear me gasping for air.

"Anna?" Julia calls out, her voice only slightly breathless. We stand silent, waiting for a reply, but none comes.

As we inch closer to the end of the hall, I can hear my heart beating in my ears. I have no idea what waits on the other side of the door, but it can't be good. We stop just short, and Julia places her hand on the cold wood. I hold my breath as I listen for any sign of life on the other side. After a few moments of silence, we lock eyes and give each other a nod. The door creaks open, and my jaw falls open as I take in the room.

Loose papers cover the floor haphazardly like a thin sheet of snow. Shelves have been ripped from the walls and broken to reveal jagged shards of wood. I look over to the marble fireplace and notice large chunks of marble have been chipped away, and the chair I sat in during my induction into the group has been turned on its side, revealing rips in the fabric like someone sliced into it with a sharp knife.

Usually, this room is brighter at this time of the morning, but whoever did this made sure to pull the floor-to-ceiling curtains closed to block out the light. Julia runs over to join Anna, Jackson, and Claire, who stand on the far end of the room, frozen in place like statues. They're staring at something. I can't see what it is, but my body goes cold as ice when Julia collapses to the ground, her scream piercing the air.

CHAPTER
FIFTEEN
LOGAN

dash over to Julia, nearly slipping on one of the papers littering the floor. I collect myself before looking down at the paper that almost sent me flying. My breath catches in my throat when I recognize the tired, forlorn expression staring back at me.

Sean Reynolds.

The *MISSING* headline stands out in bold black font, and I realize that I'm looking at the article published only yesterday.

Wow. This person works fast.

I look up from the ground and swallow the feeling of dread lodged in my throat. I step cautiously toward the group, the articles shuffling underfoot. Julia is seated on the floor, holding her knees to her chest, and Claire crouches to her level in an attempt to comfort her. I've almost made it to them when the familiar scent of blood stops me in my tracks.

———

When I woke up in the hospital after my accident, the first thing I noticed was the smell. I weakly lifted my hand to my nose and felt the dried blood that caked the inside of my nostrils. I blinked rapidly as the room came into focus, and when I tried to sit up, a searing pain passed through me like a fire burning me from the inside out. I looked around the pale walls of my hospital room and saw my mom sitting in the corner.

"Oh thank God!" she said, leaping from her seat. As she stood over me, I could see how swollen her face was. Her eyes were bloodshot, as if she hadn't stopped crying the whole time I was under.

How long had I been under?

I winced as my mom lifted me from the bed, wrapping me in a tight embrace, and she loosened her grip just enough to be bearable. Over her shoulder, I noticed a vase in the window bursting with colorful flowers. A teddy bear sat at the base, fastened by a ribbon that made it seem like the bear was holding the vase of flowers upright.

"Did Aunt Lydia send those over?" I said with a pinched tone.

My mom released me and placed a pillow behind my back to prop me up in the hospital bed. She glanced over at the flowers in the windowsill.

"No. One of your friends from school stopped by and left them for you. She said the two of you go way back." She paused, rubbing the back of her neck, clearly trying to recall the name.

My mom has always struggled with remembering names. When she would go to book signings with my dad, he would make sure to quiz her on the names of his publishing team on the way to the event to make sure she got them all right. He knew that if she got one of their names wrong, she would worry herself about it the whole ride home. This problem has only compounded as she's gotten older—it's a miracle she can remember her own name.

"Was it Emily?" I asked, watching the wheels turn in her head.

"It could have been. She told me her name, but I've been such a mess that I can't remember. Such a sweet girl to bring you these beautiful flowers. How come you never told me about her?" she asked, raising an eyebrow.

"She's just a friend, Mom." The annoyance in my voice was masked by how dry my throat felt. They must have intubated me or something, because my vocal cords felt like two pieces of sandpaper grating together.

Looking at the flowers on the windowsill, it felt good knowing Emily hadn't forgotten about me. You always make a pact with your high school best friend that you'll keep in touch when you go off to college, but then you get swept up in the newness of everything and inevitably leave your old life behind. Frankly, after everything that happened, I can't blame her for trying to forget.

Lying there in that hospital bed, I felt like a mere prisoner of my past, forced to stay behind and watch everyone else move toward their futures. I was trapped, and my broken body was a cage.

———

"There, there, Julia. It's okay. It's not a real dead body," Claire says in a kindergarten teacher's voice.

I look up from where Julia is sitting to the wall in front of me, and my hand jumps by reflex to cover my mouth, which is hanging open. The wall is covered in the same articles that cover the floor, illuminated by a ring of candles.

In the middle of the candles is what looks like a body covered in a large sheet with splotches of dark red. In the center of the chest, a large butcher knife—like one you would see in a Halloween movie—has been shoved through the sheet. Half of the blade has disappeared into the mass below, leaving the hilt standing upright. The same dark red substance pools around the blade, spreading to create one large, life-ending stain.

"It's just some asshole trying to scare us." Jackson announces smugly before walking over to lift the sheet, revealing the head of the mannequin on the floor. "I checked before I called Anna over here."

"Wait," Julia says with a sniffle as Claire helps her from the ground. "You—looked at it? What if it had been a real person under there?"

"Well then I would have gotten rid of it," Jackson adds confidently.

"Gotten rid of it, how?" Claire asks.

I watch Jackson's face as he searches for an answer. Who in their right mind would see a scene like this and have their first instinct be to look under the sheet instead of calling the police?

"I don't know. I— I was just going to play it by ear."

"Play it by ear?" Anna scoffs. "So your solution to the problem was making yourself an accomplice to murder by getting rid of the body? Seems like a great fucking plan if you ask me."

"Okay. And what would you have done, Anna?" Jackson says, his voice raised.

"How about calling the police? If someone had caught you . . ." Anna's voice trails off. She moves in close to Jackson, her mouth nearly touching the nape of his neck, and whispers something indiscernible into his ear.

I watch her with intense focus, trying to follow the movement of her lips. I miss the first few words, but I am almost certain of the rest. *Stick to the plan.*

The plan? What kind of plan could Anna be referring to? I've never seen the two of them able to hold a rational conversation for more than two minutes without it spiraling into a yelling match. How could they possibly have communicated long enough to come up with a plan? And what exactly is the plan? I have so many questions, but I don't exactly feel like being yelled at for eavesdropping, and I still have my own mission within this group. If I blow my cover too soon, I might never figure out who killed Lexi Pruitt—or even worse, I could end up like Lexi myself.

Our phones chime, the sound absorbed by the stone walls. A pit forms in my stomach when I see a text from our mystery stalker.

Make sure to smile for your mugshots :)

Suddenly, the main room of the library is filled with the sound of approaching sirens.

Shit. Are the police about to come in here and see the five of us standing around what looks like a dead body? It will be easy for them to realize that there are no actual dead bodies here, but with the sudden disappearance of Sean Reynolds, the flyers that litter the floor, and the knife jutting out of a bloody sheet, it still doesn't look great for us.

And then there's that smell. Sure, the body isn't real, but the dark splotches that cover the sheet certainly resemble real blood. One thing is for sure, I don't want to be found here when the police barge in, but where can we go? Judging by the source of the sound, they'll be coming in from the main entrance. We would just run right into them on the way out. My pulse quickens, and the feeling of dread returns to my throat.

"Quick. Follow me," Anna announces, walking over to what used to be the sitting area, stationed by the shattered marble fireplace. She approaches the small bookshelf, which has been reduced to a large rectangular box, its shelves shattered on the ground below. She gives Jackson a look before waving her hands over the wooden fragments, and he begins sliding them carefully out of the way. When the floor is clear, Anna places her high heel shoe on the bottom piece of wood, applying pressure until there's a loud click that sounds like it's coming from the other side of the wall. She grabs the left side of the book case, pulling it toward her. The base screeches against the floor, revealing a door-sized hole in the wall behind.

I catch myself staring and remind myself to pick my jaw up from the floor.

A secret entrance?

My eyes dart around the group, analyzing their reactions, but they seem just as shocked by this as I am, which tells me that up until this moment, the only one who knew about it was her.

"We can get out this way. Go," she says, flicking her head toward the exit. I want to move, but my feet feel like they're frozen to the floor.

"*Now.* Unless you want to be in here to answer the police's questions."

Jackson is the first to move, making his way down the stairs until he disappears from view. Claire is next, followed by Julia, and I go last. Once we've all started our descent, I can hear the sound of the bookcase grinding against the floor and shutting with another click, leaving us in the dark.

When we all make it to the bottom of the stairs, Anna moves to the front, taking the lead in the dimly lit tunnel. I walk closely behind Julia, my hand on the wall next to me to keep my balance. The floor below us consists of metal grates lying atop packed dirt, and the walls are covered with old boards and tarps.

I wonder about the purpose of this tunnel. Maybe it was some kind of storm shelter that never got finished or an emergency exit of some sort. But why would someone want to hide it?

We follow the tunnel until I see sunlight beaming through a metal gate in the distance. The wet ground squishes beneath my feet, and I realize we're inside one of the storm drains on campus.

We reach the end of the tunnel and file through the metal gate one at a time, and I squint as the morning light enters my eyes.

Once they've adjusted, I realize we're standing outside the storm drain, next to the library. This is the metal gate I heard clanging the day of our first meeting. I never located the culprit, but now I can't help but wonder if it was one of the Ghost Writers coming and going by way of a secret tunnel.

I groan as we climb the hill up from the storm drain. When we make it to the top, the rest of the campus comes into view, bustling with its usual morning energy.

"We were never here. Understood?" Anna says,

running her fingers through her hair. "We were not in the library this morning, and we will all go to class and pretend everything is fine, and soon this will all blow over."

I stand in silence, waiting for one of the other members of the group to ask any one of the questions I'm dying to know the answer to, but unfortunately, that doesn't happen.

"Understood?" Anna says again, this time with a firmer tone.

I nod, and the rest of the group does the same. Once Anna has confirmed the plan, she turns without another word and walks off, quickly blending into the hustle and bustle of campus this time of day. The others leave as well, and soon I'm standing alone, dumbfounded.

I pull my phone out of my pocket and see that I'm fifteen minutes late for my first class, so I decide to just use one of my allowed absences and call it a wash. My next class isn't for two hours, so I make my way back over to the coffee shop. I have too many questions to count, and it's high time I get some answers.

CHAPTER
SIXTEEN
LOGAN

can't stop my leg from shaking during Professor Alexander's lecture.

I tap on my phone and see that thirty minutes of this class has passed, and I can't recount a single thing he has said. It's been a full twenty-four hours since we got that text from Anna to rush over to the Old Library, and I haven't stopped thinking about it since.

I searched for two full hours yet could find nothing online about a secret passage into the library. I even found some old blueprints, but the stairs leading down to the long corridor we traversed yesterday were nowhere to be found.

How did Anna know about it? Did she discover it on her own, or did someone show it to her? Judging by the shocked expressions on the group's faces yesterday, Anna was the only one. If not, then these people are better liars than I initially thought. Does our secret stalker know about this entrance, and if they do, why would they have taken the time to cut the chain wrapped around the front door?

My head is swimming with all these theories and questions when the door to the classroom opens, pulling me from my trance. A frail woman walks in, and I recognize her as Debbie, Dean Aldridge's assistant. Today, she's sporting a violet dress suit with a flower embroidered on the collar, and her glasses match the ensemble perfectly. Her hair is in the same style as when she summoned me to the dean's office on my first day here; the only thing different about her is the expression of concern that forms deep wrinkles in her face.

My stomach immediately turns at the sight of her.

This is it.

I've been on edge since the moment the Ghost Writers parted ways yesterday. I can't shake the feeling that something was coming for me, and it was only a matter of time. I take some deep breaths, trying to calm my nerves as I watch her take feeble steps toward the front of the classroom.

Professor Alexander has stopped his lecture, and he meets her halfway. All eyes are on them. I watch as she pulls a slip of paper from her notebook and hands it over to him. The professor takes it, reading intently. When he's finished inspecting the note, his eyes meet mine for only a second, but the knots in my stomach are nearly unbearable.

I grab my phone in an attempt to text the group about what's happening, but I'm not fast enough.

"Logan," Alexander says, his voice carrying throughout the room, "Dean Aldridge needs to see you in his office. Debbie will escort you."

I stand from my desk, tucking my phone into my pocket as she chimes in, "Bring your things, dear. This may take a while."

Okay. Now I'm really panicking.

I pack my things into my bag, feeling every pair of eyes boring into me. When I've finally collected everything, I walk over to the door, attempting to not seem as guilty as I feel. The body we found yesterday in the library wasn't a body at all, so technically I didn't flee the scene of a murder. Do they think I had something to do with vandalizing the place?

I swallow hard and force my legs to carry me to the door, where Debbie is waiting patiently. When we met on the first day of school, she was so chatty, asking me questions about myself and talking about how excited she was to have me here at Westview, but now, as we walk down the hallway, she doesn't utter a word. The halls are silent save for the clicks of her purple heels against the floor.

I don't want to ask any questions that make me look guilty, but my nerves get the best of me, and I speak first.

"Is something wrong?" I ask, looking for any change in her expression, but there isn't any. We make it halfway before she finally responds.

"I'm not supposed to say anything," she whispers, looking up and down the hall, "but the police are here, and they just want to ask you a few questions."

Thankfully, even in the midst of what I now know is a police investigation, Debbie still loves to gossip, and the fact that she even shared that much information with me tells me she still trusts me.

Everything is going to be okay, I think to myself.

I'm not sure how much I believe it, but no matter what, I will know more in a matter of minutes.

I take a seat outside of the dean's office, and Debbie steps inside to let whoever is waiting for me inside know that I've been retrieved.

After a few moments, the door opens, and I look up, expecting to see Debbie, but instead it's a man dressed in a police uniform. He's tall and broad, with a head of salt-and-pepper hair that's short on top and shaved around the sides to create a fade effect. The name *Scott* has been embroidered into a strip of fabric and attached to the right shirt pocket, which sports a gold police badge.

"Logan," he says in a calm voice, "you can come on in."

I stand from the chair, and my legs feel weak underneath me. I know that once I enter this office, I will leave either relieved or in handcuffs. I block out the second possibility as best I can and will myself forward. We make our way into the back office. Dean Aldridge stands from his desk, gesturing to one of the two empty chairs that match the ones in the hall outside. I take my seat, and the officer closes the door before taking his place next to me.

"I don't want you to worry," Officer Scott says in a calm tone. "This is just a routine questioning, and if at any moment you feel uncomfortable, you can stand up and walk out of here."

I would love to get up and walk out at this very moment, but if I leave now, I could miss out on crucial information that might be of use in my own investigation. So I stay.

"Logan, this is Officer Scott. He is here on campus because there was a break-in at the Old Library yesterday morning."

Breathe in. Breathe out.

I repeat those words to myself over and over. My dad's life was built around researching killers, and often I would find him in his study, watching recordings of old courtroom hearings. I asked him about it, and he told me you can learn a lot from someone if you know their mannerisms when they're experiencing fear. Police use it all the time during an interrogation—asking the hard questions and watching the suspect fidget with their hands or their eyes darting around the room, desperate to look anywhere but at them.

With my dad studying up on what gave all of his subjects away, it didn't take long for him to start using his newfound skills on me. I never got away with anything growing up. Apparently, he could always tell I was lying when I would suddenly put my hands into my pockets.

I press my palms onto my thighs, making sure that they stay put as Officer Scott chimes in.

"The break-in was reported yesterday around eight in the morning, so we're asking all students who weren't in class during the time of the incident if they saw anything suspicious happening around that time."

"I didn't see anything," I manage to muster.

Officer Scott stares at me for a moment, no doubt looking for some clue as to whether I'm telling the truth or not. He breaks his gaze and lifts a piece of paper from the desk, scanning each line until he finds what he's looking for.

"Is there a reason you missed your first class yesterday?" he asks before placing the paper back on the desk.

My stomach drops. It was one thing to know that I was one of hundreds of students who weren't in class during the time of the break-in. It's another to find out I'm on an even shorter list of those who skipped their first class. I wonder how many names are on that list. I want so badly to look at the piece of paper on the desk, but I hold eye contact as I give my answer.

"Oh. I overslept and missed my first class. I set my alarm for p.m. instead of a.m."

"I can't say I haven't been guilty of doing the same thing a time or two," he says, leaning back into his seat and crossing his arms over his chest. "My wife used to tell me that it's a subconscious signal from your body that you need to rest. They must be working you really hard here at Westview." He nods toward Dean Aldridge.

The dean sits up straight in his chair, adjusting his tie slightly. "We provide challenges for our students here at Westview to better prepare them for the fast pace of the real world. We want our students to thrive not only—"

"I'm just yanking your chain, Dean," Officer Scott interjects, waving his hand. The dean relaxes back into his seat.

Officer Scott flashes a smile before reaching into his shirt pocket, then pulls out a small rectangle and holds it out to me. "If you hear anything around campus, give me a call, Logan. And while you're at it, double check that alarm tonight before you go to bed."

I take the card from him. There's a police emblem printed in the top right corner above the name Jerry Scott and a phone number at the bottom. I tuck the card into my pocket as he stands from his chair. I do the same, throwing my bag over my shoulder. I reach my hand out to the officer and he takes it, giving it a firm shake.

Debbie escorts me out of the dean's office, and the only thing I can think about is how thankful I feel to not be in shackles. Debbie gives a small wave, but before I can walk away, she places a hand on my shoulder.

"I am so sorry about all of this, Logan. We know you wouldn't have anything to do with something so heinous."

My ears perk up at her words. Officer Scott was tight-lipped with information, but I know that Debbie isn't like him, so I play into her incessant need to gossip.

"How heinous is the thing that happened?" I say, acting clueless.

"Well, they're still running tests to confirm, but—" She pauses, looking toward the door, before leaning in to whisper, "But they think the blood they found in the library matches a missing person. They're just here questioning anyone who could have seen something until the results come back."

Blood.

I knew I recognized that horrible smell. I just assumed that it was pig blood or something. I didn't think it would actually be *human* blood. Did it belong to Sean, or was it from someone else who has fallen prey to our mystery stalker?

I can feel my pulse starting to quicken, and Debbie must notice the color draining from my face. If this person is bold enough to kill someone and place the evidence in plain sight to frame us, what horrible thing could they do next? And when? The more I think about it, the harder it feels to take in a full breath of air.

"I hope they get to the bottom of it soon," I start with as brave a face as I can muster. "If I can do anything else to help, let me know."

Debbie gives a nod, a smile forming creases in her face. I watch as she makes her way back into the dean's office, and when the door clicks shut, I finally relax. I check my watch to see that my last class of the day ended about ten minutes ago, so I head toward my dorm.

Thoughts swirl in my head, drowning out the noise of a busy campus. I'm tempted to walk by the Old Library but decide against it. It was suspicious enough that I wasn't in class during the time of the incident; it would only make it worse to be seen outside of the crime scene directly after being questioned by the police.

When I make it to my room, the sun has just started to set in the sky, sending rays of yellow and orange through the sealed window. I throw my bag to the floor and take my place on the bench by the window. I'm tempted to continue looking for more information, but after yesterday's session ended at a dead end, I'm not feeling hopeful that I'll discover anything of note. I stare out through the glass, watching students trickle into their building under the watchful eye of the angel fountain.

When I first moved into this room, I looked at the fountain as a symbol of protection, but looking at her now, after everything that has happened, she seems to be warning me —telling me to cut my losses and get out while I still can. The sun is nearly set when I stand from the bench and hop in the shower. While I'm in there, I can hear my phone buzzing against the counter of the sink. The group chat is blowing up, probably talking about the next meeting and what our next move is in this investigation. It isn't until I get out of the shower to look at my phone that I realize I am very wrong.

I scroll through my notifications, catching up on the group chat. From what I can tell, the group has been trying to get a hold of Julia with no luck. Once I make it back to the top of the chat, my heart drops in my chest.

It's a new message from User125249—and it's addressed to Julia.

CHAPTER
SEVENTEEN

Hello Ghost Writers!

I hope you all aren't getting too comfortable. Since my last check-in, you all have gotten absolutely nowhere with your "investigation" into Lexi's death. Honestly, I expected more from you. This would all be so easy if you just turned yourselves in for what you did, but I guess we're going to have to continue to do this the hard way.

Now we know Jackson is a cheater and Claire is a druggie, but what do we know about everyone's favorite, bashful Ghost Writer, Julia? Sure she seems soft on the outside, but don't let that soft exterior fool you. She has been harboring a HUGE secret for someone very close to her. Curious to know more?

Julia's father, Officer Jerry Scott,

has become somewhat of a public figure in recent years. The local papers all rave over how much "heart" he has and how much he gives back to his community. This same community wonders how he is able to balance such a busy work life and still manage to be the "perfect family man." It amazes me sometimes how much you can change the image of your life, especially with social media being the new norm. One fake smile here. A family photo on the beach there. You can make even the most mundane of lives look like the rockstar lifestyle.

Unfortunately, despite what the media may want you to believe, this "perfect family man" may not be so perfect after all. I want to take you all back to two years ago, when Officer Scott's wife, Loraine Scott, made major news after a very public and violent breakdown in the local grocery store. News articles report that following an offhand comment someone made about her husband, Loraine Scott went over the edge and, when she came to, found herself holding the bystander hostage with the broken end of a wine bottle.

Following the incident, she has since stopped appearing at community events where Officer Scott is present, which has the community wondering: Where is Lorraine Scott? Some speculate that she has been placed by her family in a mental hospital to receive the treatment she needs. Others say that she's just holed up in the house, too ashamed to show her face in public. The good ole boys at the bar say he divorced her and that they don't blame him. I mean, who would want to be married to a crazy bitch like that?

While yes, on paper, her actions were grotesque and quite uncharacteristic of the kind of person we believed her to be, perhaps instead of speculating on the outburst that led to her excommunication, we should look at the root of the problem. Attached to this article, I have taken the privilege of providing a few photos I found—you know, just lying around ;)

You might recognize the woman in the photos to be none other than Lexi Pruitt's mother. Officer Scott and Miss Pruitt used to be old friends back in their college days, but when you look at those photos, I want you to ask yourself a question. Do friends typically sneak off to have sex with their friends? If that's the case, I've been doing friendships wrong my entire life.

Also, notice the date on the pictures: 8/17/2021

This picture was taken almost an entire year before Loraine snapped and attempted to stab someone in a stupor of rage. So, how long was this affair really going on? One might think that Loraine would have gotten suspicious after all of the late nights at the office turning into her husband coming home and smelling like another woman.

Even if she did know, she continued to play the part. She continued to put on her porcelain mask and smile for all of the cameras to keep up the look of having the perfect family. The longer the affair continued, the more that porcelain mask began to chip and crack, and at the end of the day, there is only so much someone can take until the mask finally shatters.

Yours truthfully
   -User 125249

CHAPTER
EIGHTEEN

JULIA

I will never forget the day I found out about my father's affair. I had just gotten out of my last class of the day, and I was in dire need of caffeine. That night was going to be a late one, since I'd decided to wait until the last minute to start writing a paper for my composition class. I could have stopped by the coffee shop on campus, but their coffee couldn't hold a candle to the local cafe in town. As I pulled up, the first thing I noticed was the police car parked on the street outside. My dad sometimes worked late at night, so it was a happy coincidence that we happened to be there at the same time, and I knew I could swindle a free coffee out of him.

I parked my car on the street across from the cafe and looked over to the large row of windows that predominately made up the street-facing side of the shop. I wanted to make sure my dad was in there before I decided to "accidentally" leave my wallet in the car. My eyes fell on my dad, decked out in his uniform, sitting at one of the tables next to the far left window. I felt a twinge in my chest when I noticed a woman who looked so familiar, but I couldn't seem to place her. I assumed they were friends from the way she was laughing at one of my dad's jokes, and I watched them interact for a bit. Before I know it, ten minutes had passed and she was standing from the table. I watched as my dad followed her out to the white Mitsubishi parked behind his. She got into her car, and my dad scanned his surroundings before leaning into the passenger-side window. I couldn't make out what they were saying, but my heart nearly stopped when I saw her lean forward and kiss him.

My dad was cheating on my mom, and I had just caught him in the act. Before he even had a chance to raise himself from the passenger window, I threw the car into gear and drove away. The entire drive home, I felt like I was in some sort of dream sequence. What I'd just witnessed wasn't real, and any minute now, I would wake up from this nightmare. Unfortunately, I never did.

That night, I took it upon myself to do some digging. I kept trying to think of where I knew this woman from, and finally it clicked. I recalled her frequent attendance at any event where my dad was present. There was one event honoring him for ten years of service where she was formally introduced to me as Adelaide Pruitt-Reynolds. With that small piece of information and a few minutes on social media, I was quickly able to find her. My face burned hot with rage. This woman had somehow worked her way into the middle of my parents' marriage, and if my mom found out about this, my life as I knew it would change forever.

I clicked around on her profile for a bit and saw that she had a family of her own. Her profile picture showed her standing next to a lanky, tired-looking man and a younger girl who shared a lot of her features, who I only could assume was her daughter. I couldn't wrap my head around the fact that both my dad and this woman had families of their own yet seemed to be hellbent on blowing them up.

The morning after I found out about my father's affair, I was sitting in the courtyard outside of the newly built library, visibly upset, disheveled, the tears that streamed down my face leaving small water stains on my pleated skirt.

I sat there thinking of all the things I would do if I ever came face-to-face with this woman. I've never been one to be confrontational, but I felt like with enough practice, I could successfully pull it off without stuttering over my words.

My phone was in my hand, and I just stared at the picture of the woman and the family that she was lying to. The anger seeping from my eyes could have burned a hole into the screen.

"Hey. Are you good?"

The words snapped me from my trance, and I quickly tried to wipe my face in an attempt to appear a little more put together. When my puffy eyes finally met my greeter, I felt myself holding my breath in disbelief.

Here she was. Right in front of me. The girl who refused to fake a smile in the very picture I'd been looking at moments before.

Lexi Pruitt.

I continued to stare at her like she was nothing more than a figment of my imagination. Like all of my emotions had personified into a hallucination that now stood in front of me. I must have stared for too long without speaking, because she awkwardly cleared her throat and spoke again.

"Sorry if I'm bothering you. I just noticed you were crying over here by yourself and wanted to make sure you were okay."

"Oh . . . sorry."

"What are you sorry for?"

"Uh. Nothing. Sorry."

"You apologize a lot."

"Yeah. Um. I guess I do. I'm fine. Just had a rough night last night. Family stuff."

"I get it. Families can be the worst. You want to talk about it? We can bitch to each other about our parents."

I watched in disbelief as she took her bag off her shoulder and took her place on the bench next to me. Not only had the daughter of the woman I'd been cyber-stalking for the past twelve hours happened to appear right in front of me, but she wanted to sit and talk. I couldn't help but wonder if she knew who I was—and what her mom had been doing out late at night with my dad.

Was all of this just a ploy to see what I knew, or was she genuinely interested in talking to me?

I've never really been one to have a lot of friends. Small talk has always been such a hard thing for me, and I'm always so wrapped up in making a good first impression that I tend to ramble or say the wrong thing and scare people off.

This conversation with her felt different. Here she was, opening up about her less-than-appealing home life to a complete stranger. As she spoke, the sounds of people bustling through the courtyard faded to the back, and I could feel the tension in my shoulder releasing and the heat leaving my face. When it was my turn to contribute to the conversation, there was a sort of natural ease that I rarely felt when talking to someone I had just met. I opened up about how I had just found out that my dad was having an affair, making sure to leave out the details that it was with this girl's mother.

"Man. That's fucked up!" she said, leaving no inclination that she knew about the skeletons lurking in her mom's closet.

I checked my watch and realized I had lost track of time and only had about five minutes to book it across campus to my next class. She must have noticed the panic starting to bloom on my face, because she reached out her hand to me.

"Here. Give me your phone."

I hesitated, then proceeded to quickly close out of social media and place my phone in her hand.

After a few seconds, she handed it back to me with a smirk.

"I saved my number in case you want to continue our conversation."

I gave her a smile and an awkward nod before placing the phone back into my bag and heading off toward my next class. I managed a few steps before turning on my heel to speak.

"It was really nice talking to you, um—"

"Lexi."

"Lexi," I echoed back to her. "My name's Julia."

"Well it was a pleasure bitching with you too, Julia. We should do it again sometime."

I gave another awkward nod and began my brisk walk across campus. The whole way to class, I couldn't shake the smile that had glued itself to my face. My mood had taken a complete one-eighty due to the kindness of a stranger. I knew from that moment on that my life wouldn't be the same. And I was right.

The days that followed included a lot of texting back and forth. It was mostly small talk, which I usually loathed, but with Lexi, it just felt natural. We would occasionally meet up for coffee and chat about all of the mundane things happening in our lives.

I remember one particular morning, Lexi and I were grabbing coffee before our first class of the day, and she mentioned how she had started a writing group on campus whose sole purpose was to seek out the truth. She hated how much all of the stuff that was being reported on around town were fluff pieces written by people who were getting paid off to spin a story in favor of the highest bidder. She wanted to tell the truth, and she knew that just like with anything in life, to tell the truth, you had to go rogue.

I could have sat there for hours and just listened to her ramble on about conspiracies and how the government was just a construct, but I was pulled out of my trance when she asked me if I would be interested in being a part of her rogue group of writers.

"M-me? You want me to join?"

"Why not? Are you not fed up with having to always put up a facade? It has to be exhausting being the daughter of such a 'highly renowned officer of the law.'"

She wasn't wrong. I had lost count of how many people I was forced to interact with at parades, social gatherings, and most recently, campaigning events for Mayor Flores. I didn't know what it was about that man that made my skin crawl.

"I have two friends I started the club with last year,

Jackson and Anna, and our goal is to recruit two new members in our second year. Anna is already bringing some girl she met at a party. I think her name was Claire? So, if you decide to join, we'll have our fifth member!"

I sat there pondering her offer. I'd never really been a part of a group before. Growing up, I was pretty clumsy, so sports weren't an option, and none of the non-sports groups really interested me. I just kept my head down and did what was asked of me through most of my life. It seemed to be working out well so far, and I wasn't sure I was ready to veer from that path to join a group of rogue writers.

"Just think about it," Lexi said as she placed her hand on top of mine, sending an electric jolt through my body. For someone who maintained such a rugged facade, her hand was incredibly soft against mine. All I could do was manage a nod and tell her I would think about it.

Later that evening, I arrived back home to the sound of the TV playing loudly from our quaint living room. When I turned the corner, I saw that it was one of those shows that people go on to take a paternity test to find out if they are or are not the father of the child in question. I had seen shows like this before and imagined that they had to be scripted. My mother detested them. She always thought there was no way someone would voluntarily air their dirty laundry on national TV the way these people did.

When I pulled my eyes from the screen, I noticed my mother was sitting on the couch.

No. Not sitting.

She had fallen asleep upright on the couch, her hand lifelessly clasped around a wine glass, which had spilled over, leaving a dark red stain on the gray cushion below. The bottle on the coffee table sat empty, and the cork had managed to roll onto the floor next to the TV remote and a receipt for Joe's Wine and Spirits with today's date on it.

I had never seen my mother have more than half a glass of wine, much less an entire bottle. I reached down and grabbed the remote, turning the volume down on the TV. I assumed that she had just innocently fallen asleep, but when I went to remove the wine glass from her hand, there was no fight. No dramatic jolting awake like she was prone to when she was woken from her sleep. Instead, her body remained motionless except for the slow rise and fall of her chest. I'd never felt so happy to see someone breathing.

Why would she drink so much on a school night?

Before I could even finish asking myself the question, the answer hit me like an arrow piercing my heart.

She knew about the affair.

Why else would she be watching a show that she hated that just so happened to do with cheaters being caught on national television? Why else would she have chosen to drink until she passed out?

I grabbed the large wool blanket that was draped over the back of the couch and laid it over my mom. I went into the kitchen to grab a damp towel and some stain remover. Mom always used to tell me that if you let a stain dry, you'll have a harder time getting it out. I sprayed the stain remover over the spot and let it sit for a moment. Then I began dabbing at it, another trick I learned from her: dab, don't rub.

After working on the stain for about ten minutes, it was as good as it was going to be. Sure, you could still see it faintly, but only if you were really looking closely. I sat on the floor of my living room and just looked at my mother. This was the first time I ever saw the strong woman who had raised me look so weak and vulnerable. I wondered how long she had known. Had she known the whole time, and was the weight of the secret finally catching up to her?

Who knew what I would have been doing right then if Lexi hadn't come to the rescue that day in the courtyard? I was able to lift the burden of what my dad had done by talking to someone about it, but my mom—who did she have?

She didn't want to bring it to me, probably to protect me from what I already knew. And all of her friends were just wives of the other police officers my dad worked with. She couldn't tell all the wives who believed her marriage to be perfect. They loved to gossip, and if word of this got out, it would ruin the man she hated, the man she still loved in spite of everything.

She had no one.

It was at that moment that I decided I would join Lexi's group of writers. I saw what lying was doing to my family, and I was ready to tell the truth.

As time went on, my mother went through phases. There would be weeks where she seemed like her normal self, and other weeks where she could hardly find the energy to get out of the bed. Eventually, the bad weeks started to outnumber the good weeks, until she found herself holding a broken bottle of wine to a stranger's neck.

When my mom hadn't come home from the grocery store that night, I knew something was wrong. My dad looked at me with glossy, tired eyes and said, "Your mom just needs some time away to recharge."

I knew there was more he wasn't telling me, and it wasn't hard to find the details of what had happened since the incident was plastered all over social media. I later came to find out that she had been charged with attempted murder, but thanks to good ole Officer Scott, she was able to plead insanity to a court of her peers and was sentenced to spend six months to a year working with a psychiatrist to help her learn better coping strategies at a "resort" a few towns over.

It took some adjustment coming home to an empty house every day. Even if the house wasn't empty, and my dad happened to be home at a decent hour, I would just hide away in my room and barely acknowledge his existence.

The distance that had grown between my father and me didn't go unnoticed. One Friday, he came home late from work and must have seen that my lamp was still on in my room. Lexi and I would often find ourselves texting at all hours of the night, which was a great distraction from my nearly solitary home life. Talking to her was like being encased in a bubble of light in the midst of a vast, empty darkness.

The knock on the door startled me, and I tried to quickly roll over to pretend I had fallen asleep with the lamp on, but I wasn't fast enough. When my dad entered the room, it was the first time I noticed how tired he truly looked. The purple splotches that plagued the space under his eyes made him look like someone had given him a couple of black eyes. He had lost weight, and the usual rosy color that filled his cheeks had faded to a pale pink.

I didn't know what I could possibly say, so I didn't say anything at all. He walked over to my bed, his heavy work boots thudding on the hardwood floor with each step, and slowly lowered himself to sit on the edge of my bed. For a long stretch we sat there in silence, and I watched as he stared at the floor, preparing whatever speech I was about to get.

"I'm so sorry, Julia," he mustered through a clenched throat.

Sorry? Was that really all he had to say for everything?

"This is all my fault," he continued. "I never meant for any of this to happen, and I know you probably hate me, especially with everything that has happened with your mother—what I've done to her. She didn't deserve any of this."

Tears rolled down my face. I was so angry at him. I didn't understand why he would do this. But also, at this moment, I couldn't help but feel pity for him. Just like my mother, he always had a strong jubilant facade, and the same mask that she wore was now also missing from his drooping face.

"I don't hate you, Dad," I said, wiping the tears from my face. "But I don't understand. Why would you do this? Do you and Mom not love each other anymore?"

A sad smile broke across his face. "I wish it were that simple. Please just know that this has nothing to do with your mother and everything to do with—"

"Are you still seeing her?"

My dad turned to me, his eyes wide as he came to the realization that I knew everything. I knew about the affair, the incident with my mom, all of it.

"No. I'm not still seeing her. It was a mistake, and I will spend the rest of my life making it up to you and your mom. I promise."

With those final words, he let out a groan and lifted himself back to his feet. He stopped in the doorway and gave me one last tired smile before walking out and closing the door behind him. I listened as the sound of his boots faded down the hallway, until I was sure I was alone again.

I pulled my phone out from under the blanket and saw a message from Lexi.

Did you fall asleep on me again?

I smiled and replied.

No. Just had a weird conversation with my dad. But I probably should be getting to sleep soon. Got a big test tomorrow.

In just a few seconds, her response came.

Oooo sounds juicy. Talk about it over coffee tomorrow?

I wrote back, unable to keep a smile from forming on my lips.

It's a date :)

———

I stare at the screen of my phone with conflicted emotions. On one hand, I'm devastated for my mom, who will no doubt have to answer a million questions in her fragile state should this article see the light of day. On the other hand, I feel relieved. I've been harboring this for so long, and the longer I carried this secret for my family, the heavier it became to hold.

When something bad happens to us, we think it's the end of the world should our peers find out, but I believe life's most challenging moments create the best and strongest people. Lexi was one of those people. Her home life was a wreck, but behind all of that pain was one of the most beautiful souls I have ever had the pleasure of encountering. I would have done anything to protect her from what happened that night. If only I had looked at my phone sooner, maybe Lexi would still be alive.

The thing about the words "what if" is how deeply they can bore themselves into your soul. Something tragic happens, and you can't help but wonder if it could have been prevented had you acted faster—or not at all.

What if my dad never had the affair?

What if I'd seen Lexi's text sooner?

What if I'd been brave enough to let go of my dad's secret?

I will have to deal with "what if" for the rest of my life, but I will not let some asshole scare me into submission. I will find out what happened that night for Lexi, and I can't wait to look the culprit in the face and tell them how they took everything from me. I want them to feel the pain I feel every day, having lost the person I trusted more than anyone else in this world.

CHAPTER
NINETEEN
LOGAN

I awake the following morning to the sound of my phone pinging on the nightstand. I sit up in bed, attempting to rub the sleep from my eyes, already thinking of the coffee I'll need in order to survive the day.

I stayed up entirely too late last night. I found myself looking into the incident mentioned in User125249's most recent article. I found the original article covering the brutal encounter involving Loraine Scott. I've checked my phone periodically to see if Julia reached out, but she's kept a low profile. I wanted to reach out myself, but being so new to the group, I figured one of the other Ghost Writers would be more qualified to come to her aid.

I gain my bearings in the room, now illuminated by the morning sun, before reaching over and unplugging my phone from its charger. The first thing I see is the time. It's eight in the morning, which means I slept for a total of four hours last night. Today should be fun.

My heavy eyes grow wide when I see a notification from Julia, and I tap on the message.

I want to find out what drugs were in
Lexi's system when she died . . . but I'll
need help.

She doesn't even mention the article exposing her family secret, and I can't help but wonder if she's seen it. She has to have seen it. Why would this person be sending their newest article to just me? I move over to the group chat and see it has also been radio silent since the article was posted. Have any of the other Ghost Writers seen it?

I stare at the screen before throwing the covers to the side and pulling myself from the bed. I splash some water on my face and get ready for the day. The whole time, I can't help but think of Julia. I can only imagine how she feels, and a knot forms in my stomach knowing that it's only a matter of time until my name is in one of those horrible articles.

My phone pings again, just as I'm about to walk out the door. I lift the screen to see Anna's response.

I'll be there.

So short and emotionless, but I guess that's what I've learned to expect from Anna Flores. I quickly type out my response.

Me too! Whatever you need :)

By the time I'm sitting in my last class of the day, we have our plan of attack for tonight. Anna and I will drive Julia to the police station and wait outside while she gets the information she's looking for. Julia would be fine to drive, but too many people around the station know her car from the summers she worked there as an intern. I didn't have much to offer to the operation, but I will be there as emotional support. Jackson and Claire won't be in attendance, as Claire is helping Jackson study for a big test he has coming up later this week.

When I saw the message from Jackson explaining he wouldn't be there tonight, I waited for one of Anna's famous rants, but it never came. I guess being a politician's daughter taught her to never put her true feelings in writing.

Anna arrives outside my dorm at eight o'clock on the dot. The sun has fully set in the sky as I shove my phone in my pocket and zip up my dad's blue jacket. I'm not sure what we'll find tonight during what Julia has cleverly titled "Operation: Tox Screen," but just in case it isn't good news, I'll have my dad with me.

I make it to the bottom floor of my building to see the same guy working the desk, his headphone blasting in his ears. At this point, I'm not sure he actually does any work, but good for him for making money, I guess.

I find a black Tesla waiting out front. I don't know if I've ever seen a car this nice in person, much less ridden in one. The window rolls down as I approach, and I see Anna in the driver's seat.

"Are you waiting for an invitation?" she says in her usual snarky tone.

I swallow hard before opening the door and taking my place in the passenger seat. I take in the interior, and to no surprise, it's just as pristine as the outside. There's a large screen where the radio should be, and not a speck of dirt in sight. There is a hint of new-car smell, masked by a floral air freshener that blows through the vents. If I didn't know any better, I would think that this car was driven off the lot and straight here.

I close my eyes in an attempt to calm my thoughts. Dread creeps into my bones and rises up through my shoulders. Every time I get into a car, I hope that this dread will be behind me, but I'm met with the same fear. I fidget with the frayed sleeve of my jacket as we begin to move forward, and I focus on keeping my breath calm and even.

I've leveled out by the time we pick up Julia. She has one of those insulated coolers keeping the food she's prepared for her and her father warm until we arrive at the station. When she enters the car, the smell of roasted chicken fills my nose, intertwining itself with the pungent floral scent that has now triggered a headache. The pain in my head is a good distraction as the car pulls out of Julia's driveway, taking us to our destination.

When we arrive at the police station, Anna is careful to park her car on a side lot, out of view from any windows. We go over the plan once more.

Julia will go in and have dinner with Officer Scott. She'll excuse herself to go to the restroom and use that time to log into the system and pull the toxicology report on Lexi Pruitt.

With everyone in agreement, Julia makes her way into the station, cooler in tow, and Anna and I are left alone to wait.

———

It's been about an hour since Julia went inside. Anna has been on her phone scrolling or texting the entire time we've been sitting here. Every two seconds, her phone is vibrating with a new notification. I don't know who all she's been messaging with, but based on the long sigh that follows each message, it isn't someone she wants to be talking to.

I tried to start light conversation in an attempt to get to know her outside of being a . . . not nice person, but my attempts were all met with one-word answers. After the third try, I took the hint and gave up, and I've been playing one of those matching games on my phone since. It isn't the most exciting thing, but it's kept me occupied. I'm about to win the level I'm on when my phone buzzes in my hand.

Julia's name pops up at the top of my screen, and I click on the notification immediately. Anna does the same, sitting up in her seat.

> Just finished dinner. About to "go to the bathroom."

"God. Did it take her an hour just to eat?" Anna scoffs before typing furiously on her phone and slamming it face down in her lap. Half a second later, her message back to Julia pops up on my screen.

> How much longer are you going to be?
> We've been out here for over an hour.

I roll my eyes before typing my response.

> Sounds good. Be careful!

I sit and stare at the three little bubbles that let me know someone is typing, but after a minute or two, they disappear. I linger in the chat, waiting for a response, but when it doesn't come, I switch back over to my game.

I've beaten three more levels by the time a knock comes on the window. I nearly jump from my seat, and my phone flies from my hand, bouncing off the dashboard before landing at my feet.

"Hey!" Anna says. "If you could not try to crack my windshield, that'd be great."

I give an apologetic nod before turning to look out my window. A woman is standing there, dressed in her uniform. Her dark braids are pulled back into a bun, and her shirt pocket tells me her name is Williams.

Anna rolls down the window, taking away the only barrier between me and Officer Williams.

"Sorry. Didn't mean to startle you," the woman says.

"Hi, Officer," Anna says without looking up from her phone, "Can we help you?"

The officer sees Anna and immediately replaces her stern expression with a wide, toothy grin.

"Good to see you, Miss Flores. How's your father doing?"

"Oh, you know. Busy as always."

Officer Williams lets out an exaggerated chuckle, and at this point I can tell that she's trying to stay on Anna Flores's good side.

"Well, we noticed you guys have been parked outside for a while, and I just wanted to make sure everything is okay."

"Yeah, we're fine," Anna says, raising her hand at the officer. "We're just picking up a friend. She should be out any minute."

"Oh. Are you two friends of Julia's?" Officer Williams asks.

I look over to Anna, who has grown bored of this conversation and is tapping away at that screen.

Who has she been talking to this whole time?

I look back to the officer, giving a nod and a forced smile.

"Isn't that sweet. I'm so happy to meet some of Julia's friends. She had such a hard go of it last year, but she seems to be doing much better and —

"Officer Williams?" a voice calls from behind her. "Is something wrong?"

I turn my head to see Julia standing behind the officer, her cooler slung over her shoulder.

"No. Not at all. I was just meeting a couple of your friends."

Julia opens the back passenger door and sets the cooler on the seat.

"Well, I won't keep you. It was so good to see you again, Anna, and it was nice meeting you . . ."

"Logan," I say.

"Logan," she echoes. "So great to meet you. You all get home safe, alright?" She turns to wrap Julia in a hug before making her way back into the station. Julia plops down into the back seat, prompting a frustrated sigh from Anna. I roll my eyes and turn toward Julia.

"Did you find anything on the tox report?"

"I found a couple things, but I don't recognize —"

"Not here," Anna interrupts, and I snap my eyes to meet her. "Probably not a good idea to discuss the information we obtained illegally right outside the police station."

Julia and I remain silent as Anna puts the car into gear. I quickly refasten my seat belt as we pull out onto the main road, and I watch as the police station grows smaller in the rearview mirror. Once it's disappeared into the distance, Julia pulls her phone from her bag and starts tapping on the screen.

"Okay, so according to the tox report, Lexi had two substances in her system at the time she died. I recognize the antidepressants, but the other thing I've never heard of."

"What's it called?" I ask as I open the web browser on my phone.

"Albuterol. Not sure I'm saying it correctly. Here, look." Julia holds out her phone, and I scan the screen until I find the name. I copy it into my browser and click on the first link that pops up.

"Albuterol," I begin reading aloud, "is used to prevent and treat wheezing, difficulty breathing, chest tightness, and coughing caused by lung diseases such as asthma and —"

Suddenly, Anna slams on the brake, jolting us all forward in our seats and prompting the car behind us to blare their horn. I close my eyes and brace myself in the seat as Anna whips the car into the parking lot directly to our right. She pulls into the nearest spot and shoves the gear shift into park.

"What the hell, Anna!?" Julia calls from the back seat.

I take deep breaths as I force my eyes open and gain my bearings. If this is how Anna normally drives, I will not be making a habit of getting in the car with her in the future. Before I can speak again, Anna snatches my phone from my hands and starts scanning the page for more information. There's a panic in her eyes that I've never witnessed before, and for the first time since the cyber-stalking began, she seems truly afraid.

"Julia," she says, her voice shaking, "what happens

when this drug is combined with the antidepressants Lexi was taking?"

Julia types the two substances into her search engine and begins reading aloud the first article.

"Using albuterol together with antidepressants can increase the risk of an irregular heart rhythm that may be serious or potentially life threatening."

"And how does the report say that Lexi died?" Anna asks.

I watch as Julia taps on the phone, and the moment she finds what she is looking for, her face drops.

"Heart failure," she says in a grave tone.

Anna tosses my phone back to me, and I fumble around until it eventually lands in my lap. "But that's not all," Julia says in a way that can only be followed with bad news. "Forensics came back on the blood the police found in the library."

My eyes go wide, and I perk up at the potential new lead in the investigation.

"Sometime today would be nice," Anna demands, but neither of us are prepared for what she says next.

"The blood. It belongs to Benson."

"Benson?" Anna says. "As in Benson Wright?"

Julia nods, her lips pressed into a flat line.

The name is so familiar, but I can't seem to place it. Why would his blood be at the crime scene? Images of the mannequin covered in blood flash across my mind. There was a lot of blood there, so it was either taken out slowly over time—or Benson is dead.

My body goes cold at the thought. I knew the situation was getting dangerous, but with another possible death so close to home, I feel less safe than ever.

And what about Sean Reynolds? If the blood isn't his,

then where is he? The timing of his disappearance can't be a coincidence. There's still a chance he could be our mystery stalker, but for some reason, I can't imagine the lifeless man from the photograph being a threat to anyone.

Julia must notice how lost I look in this conversation, because she says, "Benson was the guy we were telling you about after our first meeting."

"Basically, he's a loser third-year senior who preys on younger women," Anna chimes in, her words filled with venom.

"Oh yeah. Isn't that the guy Anna saved Claire from at a party or something?"

"Yep, and then poured a drink over his head," Julia says with a smug smile.

Anna leans forward, pressing her face into the palms of her hands, and begins sobbing. I look to Julia, who seems just as shocked by this sudden outburst of emotion.

"What's wrong?" I ask.

She doesn't lift her face from her hands, but she doesn't have to. Her muffled words ring out clear as day.

"I think Claire might be our killer."

CHAPTER
TWENTY
LOGAN

"*Claire*? Why would you say that?" Julia asks.

Anna takes a moment to compose herself, dabbing under her eyes with a tissue she pulled from her purse.

"Lexi died of heart failure, and the two drugs in her system were antidepressants and asthma medication. Claire is the only one who would have access, since her family owns a pharmacy and all."

"Okay, but her medicine being found in Lexi's system doesn't instantly make Claire the killer," Julia argues.

"But don't you think it's a little suspicious that the blood in the library belongs to a guy she hates? She's the only one of us who would want to kill him. Add in the fact that her drugs were in Lexi's system, and I say it's a pretty convincing case."

I hate to admit it, but Anna is right. All of the evidence we currently have points to Claire. Her perky attitude *would* make for a great cover-up. Is that why she didn't want to be here with us at the police station? Was she afraid that we would discover her truth and she would be arrested in a matter of seconds?

Anna frantically searches for her phone in the dark car. Once she's located it, she types vigorously, her nails clicking against the screen, before lifting the phone to her ear.

"Who are you calling?" Julia asks from the back seat.

"Who do you think I'm calling?" Anna snaps, her eyes growing more frantic with each passing dial tone.

Julia and I sit quietly, listening to each ring, until the automated voicemail begins playing.

"Shit!" Anna shouts, slamming the phone down in her lap with a huff.

Based on past interactions, I would've never guessed that Anna cares this deeply for Jackson, but seeing her now in this dimly lit car with mascara trailing down her face, I'm not sure what to think.

Anna taps the screen a few more times before plugging her phone into the small cord connected to the radio. A map is displayed on the built-in screen, showing directions to the nearby recreation center. Without another word, she throws the car into gear, and I frantically buckle myself back into my seat before reaching for the bar overhead. My knuckles turn white, and I try to steady my breathing as Anna peels out of the parking lot and onto the street.

Breathe in. Breathe out.

Anna speeds forward, which is enough to make my heart palpitate out of my chest. At this time of night, the number of cars on the street has dwindled drastically, and I take solace in the fact that Anna doesn't have to weave through any traffic.

"Did Jackson and Claire tell you where they were going?" Julia asks from the back seat.

"Didn't have to. Jackson shared his location with me a while back and forgot to turn it off."

I pull up the website of the rec center and check their hours. They closed at seven, which according to the clock on my phone was three hours ago. Jackson told us that Claire was helping him study, but how did they end up at the rec center this late at night? Anna seems to be fully convinced that Claire is our resident killer, and I can't fault her logic. Claire has a pharmacy of drugs in her arsenal and is prescribed the drug that killed Lexi. The only thing missing for me is a motive, but as the newest member of the Ghost Writers, there's so much history in this group that I don't know about.

I watch the map, and the closer we get to our destination, the more nauseous I become. I feel as though I'm strapped into a roller coaster bound for an incomplete track, with no power to stop it. There's no way of knowing what waits for us at the end of this ride, but there is a pit in my stomach telling me that whatever it is, it isn't good.

Anna turns off her headlights as we pull into the recreation center parking lot. The night sky cloaks us in shadows, and the only source of light is the map glowing as we inch toward the checkered-flag symbol marking Jackson's location. According to this, Jackson should be just on the other side of the center, which stands like a miniature coliseum with a dome roof. Pictures of various sporting equipment are set aglow on the front of the building.

Anna pulls the car around the left side of the center before cutting the engine and leaving us in quiet darkness. She waits a couple of breaths before opening her door and stepping out of the car. Julia and I share a look before following her lead and joining her, our backs pressed against the side of the building. The wall is cold, sending a chill through the back of my jacket.

"What's the plan?" I whisper, my breath forming small clouds in front of my face.

"We walk up and confront her," Anna says. "It will be one versus four. There's no way she could take all of us at once."

Anna peeks around the corner toward the parking lot on the back side of the recreation center. Julia and I creep forward to do the same, and I notice two cars next to each other.

I recognize Claire's, since we rode together during the trip to her family's pharmacy. A chill goes down my spine at the thought of being alone in the car with her. If she is capable of what Anna thinks she's capable of, I could have just as easily been in the same situation Jackson is in right now.

I don't recognize the large truck and can only assume that it belongs to Jackson. The parking lot is dimly lit, and from this distance, I can't tell if there's anyone in either of the cars. I look over to Anna, who seems to be having the same amount of trouble as I am. Her eyes are locked, scanning for any sign of movement, and when she doesn't detect any, she steps from around the corner and starts walking toward the two cars.

Anna springs into action, and Julia and I follow closely behind. It would have been nice to have a warning before possibly walking toward a murder scene, but I guess I should know by now that warnings aren't really Anna's thing.

My eyes lock on to the cars, and each step closer sends a shockwave through my body telling me to turn around and run far away from here. What are we going to do if Jackson is dead? I think of what Anna will do to Claire and if I'll be a forced witness to two murders.

Anna freezes in place, and I nearly walk straight into her back. I move my eyes to see where she's looking and notice the two shadows moving inside of Jackson's truck. Anna creeps forward, watching the truck like a predator watches its prey.

Suddenly, there's a jolt within the truck, shaking the cab. I look through the windshield to see that the two shadows have now conjoined to form one large blob rustling around inside.

"She's on top of him! We have to stop her!" Anna yells, darting to the truck.

"Anna. Wait!" Julia yells as we begin running after her.

Anna pauses for a second, kicking the high heels from her feet before continuing her dash for the vehicle. We're a few steps behind her when she reaches the driver side door and yanks the handle. The door swings open, and I prepare for the gruesome scene that waits on the other side of the door. When I see Claire straddling a shirtless Jackson, my jaw nearly falls to the pavement.

Claire quickly pushes herself from Jackson's muscled torso and into the passenger seat. Jackson fumbles around for his shirt, finding it on the floorboard beneath his feet. He steps out of the car, throwing the shirt over his head and torso.

"Anna, it isn't what it looks like." Jackson steps toward Anna with an outstretched hand, causing her to retreat. She stares silently as tears begin streaming down her face, following the dark trails left behind by her breakdown earlier.

"Anna, I'm sorry. I don't know what came over me. We were just talking and—"

"How long?" Anna asks, raising a hand to cut him off.

"What?"

"How long have you been fucking her?"

Jackson's eyes lower to the dark asphalt. Without looking up from the ground, he manages to muster, "Six months."

Anna takes in a sharp breath, releasing it with a slow chuckle.

"What's so funny?" Jackson says, pulling his gaze up to meet Anna's bloodshot eyes.

"I hope you are really proud of yourself, Jackson," Anna says before turning her attention to Claire. "Good luck screwing her when she ends up in prison."

"Prison? What the hell are you talking about, Anna?" Claire says, throwing the passenger door open and stepping out of the truck.

"She killed Lexi!" Anna points her finger in Claire's direction, her voice now hysterical. "Lexi's tox screen shows she had albuterol in her system when she died. The same drug that Claire uses for her asthma."

"Are you serious, Anna? Why would you think I had anything to do with Lexi's death? She was my friend!"

"And I thought you were *my* friend, yet here you are hooking up with *my* boyfriend in the middle of a fucking parking lot! If this is how you treat your friends, then who knows what you could have done to Lexi. You are sick, Claire." Anna turns to walk back to her car.

"And you're a *bitch*, Anna!" Claire yells before she can stop herself.

Anna freezes midstep and turns to face her, a searing rage in her eyes.

"What did you just call me?" Anna's voice is a low growl.

"You're a cold, emotionless, *bitch*," Claire says, matching Anna's tone.

"Claire, stop!" Jackson demands.

"Why? She treats everyone like they're below her, including you! It's no wonder you felt the need to find someone else to take care of you. You told me yourself, Anna hasn't been intimate with you since before Lexi died."

"You stupid slut! The only reason you're here is because of *me*. I was the one who found you at that party and brought you into this group. You'd be a nobody, knocked up by whatever senior had sniffed you out first to get you on your back. And when the police find out what you did to Lexi—"

"I didn't do anything to Lexi! What part of that don't you get?! I don't know how she ended up with albuterol in her system. You can call me whatever you want, but I am not a goddamn killer! If anything, you're a killer. She probably killed herself to get away from *you*! And after everything Jackson has said about you, I can see why."

Anna releases a guttural scream and charges toward Claire with her claws bared. Jackson intervenes, creating a wall between the two as Anna continues to fight against him to no avail.

"I'm going to kill you!" Anna roars through gritted teeth. "Jackson let me go!"

Jackson winces as Anna pounds her fists into his back. I want to help, but at this point, this is way out of my domain. I honestly don't know which of the two outcomes would have been worse for Anna: the man she loves being murdered, or the man she loves betraying her.

I start to take a step forward, but I feel a hand grab mine. I turn to see Julia. Her face says *You don't want to get involved with this.* I heed her warning, staying planted in place, and watch as Anna continues to try to break free from Jackson's hold. This continues until the sound of our phones ringing in eerie harmony causes Anna to collapse in Jackson's arms.

CHAPTER
TWENTY-ONE

My beloved Ghost Writers,

I want to congratulate you on putting a large piece of the puzzle together, but this is no time to celebrate. You know the drugs that killed Lexi, but you still have no clue as to what really happened that night and the roles you all played in it. Maybe another article will motivate you to hasten your investigation.

This one is dedicated to your very own Politics Princess, Anna Flores. Yes, her father is a very powerful political figure here in Westview, and has managed to run what the community is calling one of the cleanest campaigns they've ever seen! Well I have news for every one of my readers: There is no such thing as a clean campaign when it comes to politics and power. Power is a corruptive resource. It is an addictive drug and the more you receive, the more you crave. Mayor Flores—now Governor Flores—is no different.

Mayor Flores was willing to do whatever it took to make sure his campaign ran as smoothly as possible, even if that meant hurting the people closest to him. No one was safe. Not even sweet little Anna.

Now, it is no secret that Jackson and Anna are the power couple of the century in Westview. Both of their families come from power and money, and those two things go together like peanut butter and jelly. Their relationship on the surface seemed to be a modern-day arranged marriage, but what many don't know is that their relationship actually started with love.

The two of them hated their place in their parents' plans and bonded over their distaste for social events and campaign strategies. The two of them would often be found sneaking off to the train tracks on the outskirts of Westview for hours at a time, doing God knows what. After a few of those times together, Anna began to fall ill. Her mother took her to see their family doctor and discovered that somewhere along the way, Anna had found herself with child.

If the news got out about Mayor Flores's daughter being pregnant out of wedlock, that would lead to some juicy headlines and allow for his opponents to find a soft spot in his campaign. They wouldn't think twice about hitting him where it hurt the most.

In politics, if something shines an unfavorable light on a particular candidate, the most common solution is to get rid of it, even if "it" was growing inside his only daughter.

Now, I don't want to place the blame solely on her father, because it was actually Jackson's father who fronted the bill for Anna's little procedure. If this union was to work, Mayor Flores had to maintain his power, and in order to do that, he had to win the election, which would not happen if this baby were to be brought into the world.

Not only did Anna and Jackson's family pay to get rid of the next heir to their throne, they also paid a decent sum of money to the doctor to have any documentation of the procedure shredded.

Power is quite the addictive substance, and just like with any other addiction, once you don't have it anymore, there may be a relapse of sorts.

Guess you better get to the bottom of

this, and soon, because the big finale is on the horizon, and I will make sure that each and every one of you will burn for what you did to Lexi.

See you soon :)

-User125249

CHAPTER
TWENTY-TWO
ANNA

melt from Jackson's arms into a puddle on the cold asphalt. I lift the article to my face, reading the words through burning eyes. My mind floods with memories, each painful wave crashing into the next. I've tried every day to forget, but I remember every grueling detail as if it happened yesterday.

———

"You're pregnant," Dr. Rollins said, scanning over the blue clipboard in his hands.

It was almost like someone had taken all the air out of the room, and all I could do was stare at the sign on the wall with emojis to express different levels of pain. If I had to choose, at this moment, I was feeling a level of pain beyond any that was depicted. It wasn't a physical pain. It was the kind of pain you feel in your chest when your hope is shattered. Where every plan you have ever made for yourself is a tower of glass, and two words made of stone send the entire thing falling to the ground into a pile of jagged shards. There is no hope of putting the pieces back together. There's just a hopeless mess in front of you and an endless void of pain inside.

I looked from the poster on the wall to my mother, who always seemed to know the right thing to say, but not this time. She just looked back with tearful eyes. I was uncertain whether they were tears of sadness, disappointment, or some nauseating combination of the two.

"You can stop by the front desk to set up your follow-up appointment," Dr. Rollins announced before leaving the room.

I remember sitting in that room for what felt like an eternity. I wanted my mom to say something—anything—to make me feel better like she always knew how to do. But there was nothing. She let out a long sigh and rose from her chair, throwing her designer purse over her shoulder.

"Please don't tell Dad." Those were the only words I could manage as tears began to fill my eyes.

My mother paused and looked at me, the fluorescent overhead lighting casting a shadow over her face. Really, she looked through me, because she already knew what she had to do, and she was so upset with me for putting her in this position.

When we got home, I started for the stairs, but before I could take even a few steps away, she stopped me.

"Anna," she said, her voice firm.

I turned to see her standing there with an outstretched hand. I looked down at her manicured fingers and back to her deep brown eyes, perplexed as to what she was asking me for.

"Phone," she said with little inflection.

I wanted to refuse, but I knew I was in no position to make a bargain with her. I reached into my pocket to retrieve my phone and placed it in her hand. She looked toward the stairs, which was her usual way to signal that I had been dismissed. I turned away without another word and made my way up to my room.

I lay on my bed and cried until sleep finally numbed the pain, but when I awoke, the pain returned like a wave of salt water crashing into an open wound. My face was still puffy, and judging by the lack of sunlight outside, I had slept for a few hours. My throat was dry, and I desperately needed water. I opened my door and crept down the stairs. I didn't have a clock in my room, and my mother had taken my only way to tell what time it was, but I knew it was late, because my dad was home from a long day of campaigning. He had a deep voice that could carry across a room even as a whisper, and I could hear him talking to someone in the kitchen.

At first, I thought he was talking to my mother. I didn't know what all she had disclosed to him, and I couldn't help but wonder if I had suddenly gone from daddy's little girl to daddy's little secret. I was almost to the bottom of the stairs when I heard another man's voice—one that I recognized.

It was Jackson's dad.

My mind raced as I tried to come up with a good reason for them to be at our house so late. Curious, I remained in the dark stairwell and tried my best to be a fly on the wall.

"So you see where I'm coming from, don't you?" my dad said in his politician voice.

"I do. I understand how this could affect your campaign, and in the interest of both of our families, I am more than happy to assist you however you need," Jackson's father replied.

I peeked around the corner to see the two men standing in the kitchen. The wives sat next to each other, consoling one another and keeping their opinions out of the conversation. It was an unspoken rule between our two families that when it came to political strategizing and problem solving, the women should remain seen and not heard.

I always resented that sentiment, which was part of the reason I hated all of the obligations I was required to attend. I was a prop, a pretty little thing for people to gawk at and admire and nothing more.

"Well, I think we both agree she can't keep it," my father said, inspiring another sob to escape my mother. "I also believe that once this incident is . . . resolved, it should remain between us."

"I think that is wise. There's no need for Jackson to ever know about something that never existed in the first place," Jackson's father said with a wink.

As I heard those words leave his lips, my whole body wanted to scream.

How could I possibly keep something like this from Jackson?

He would never forgive me. I pushed both hands over my mouth to keep my scream at bay. I hadn't realized how hard I was pushing until the taste of blood filled my mouth from my teeth digging into my lips. Tears rushed from my eyes. I was in no position to be a mom, but they never even gave me the option to consider it. They never gave me the option to allow this child made from love to grow inside of me and come into the world with two parents who would love it—listen to it. A sob escaped me, silencing the conversation in the kitchen.

Shit.

As quickly and quietly as I could manage, I padded up the stairs and returned to my room. I crawled into bed and lay there until sleep finally came.

A week later, I was back in Dr. Rollins's office, this time accompanied by my father. I was dressed in a paper gown, lying on the table to await my fate. My father held my hand, but not in a loving way. The tight grip of his rough hand around mine was a warning. It was a warning to me that if I were to run and continue with this pregnancy, I would no longer be considered a part of the family. I would be exiled and put out on the street or locked away somewhere in the house, and all of the pretending I had done to survive my parents would have been for nothing.

When the procedure was finished, I lay on the table for what felt like another hour. I felt numb, violated, and helpless. When I finally blinked, my eyes burned. I had no more tears left to cry.

"You need to get dressed," my father said, lifting himself from the chair that sat in the corner of the room. "We have an event tonight, and you are expected to be there."

I didn't move. I couldn't even look at him as he walked out, leaving me alone in a cacophony of silence. When I finally managed to push myself from the bed, the pain I felt in my abdomen shot through my entire body. I slowly and awkwardly removed the paper garment I had been subjected to upon arrival and wormed my way into the stack of sweats I left the house in.

As I shuffled out to the waiting room, I saw my dad talking with Dr. Rollins. I couldn't tell what he was saying, but as soon as I saw the envelope move from my father's coat pocket to Dr. Rollins's hand, I knew what had been done. He was covering his tracks. We were never here, there would be no documentation of the procedure, and in exchange, Dr. Rollins could take an early retirement from his practice. The envelope was tucked into his white coat, the two men shook hands, and we were home free.

Later that evening, I had traded my sweats for an emerald-green dress that was both elegant and comfortable on my brittle body. I sat at my vanity and stared at a reflection I didn't recognize. When a knock sounded at my door, I turned to see my mother standing in the doorway.

I looked at the woman whom I'd once admired and considered a superhero. In that moment, I saw nothing more than a weak woman whose place in this family had been decided for her. She was just a pawn in a game she didn't want to play. I almost felt sympathy for her as she looked at me with sad eyes.

I turned back to my reflection and began putting on my earrings—emerald stones wrapped in gold to match my dress. As I fastened the first one, she moved closer, but she stopped halfway between me and the door.

"I am so sorry, Anna. I tried to convince him –"

"Go," I said.

I didn't have to look at her to know she was caught off guard. She had always been the person I could confide in about everything. I'd told her about the monster that lived in my closet when I was a little girl. I'd told her about how I punched Jimmy Walters in the face after he made fun of my haircut in the seventh grade. I'd told her when I failed a test and I was afraid to tell Dad about it. I told her everything, and she always knew the answer. At the end of all of those confidential talks, she would say the same thing: "It'll be our little secret." If only this time could have been the same. When I truly needed her most, she let me down.

"Anna—"

"I said go."

Knowing she had been dismissed yet again, she backed out of the room, her heels clicking. My mother was no longer my safe space. As long as I lived in this house, I no longer had a safe space.

When we arrived at the Chateau Luxe, the location of the night's event, I stepped out of the car with a smile painted across my face in an attempt to hide the scraping pain I felt. Every step sent a jolt of electricity through my body, to the point where I felt nauseous. If I didn't find somewhere to sit down soon, I was sure I would pass out.

We passed through the lobby and made our way to the ballroom stationed in the right wing of the hotel. High ceilings held extravagant crystal chandeliers that seemed to sparkle like stars in the warm lighting. French carpet adorned every square inch of the floor, which was now sprinkled with standing cocktail tables and lounge chairs for people to sit in and gossip about all of the goings-on around the campaign. In these settings, it was all about mingling and making connections, because you never knew who among you would be the next to climb the social ladder. There were no true friendships here. Every relationship was based on a business decision.

I stood in the doorway to the ballroom, looking out at the sea of tuxes and opulent evening gowns as my father reached his hand around my right arm. When my face met his, he gave me a smile, but I knew what he was really saying behind bared teeth.

Keep it together tonight, and your little incident—as he referred to it—*will be forgiven.*

I gave a nod, and he was off to begin swooning the room with that vile charm that seemed to come so naturally to him. My mother went in the opposite direction, to the lounge area filled with the politicians' wives. They greeted each other with empty hugs, kissed each other on the cheek, and spewed empty compliments regarding each other's appearances.

I was left there alone, eyeing the room for any seat that remained available. Luckily, there were a few vacant ornate chairs placed next to each other in the back of the room. I began to make my way through the crowd, making sure to say a quick hello to those I had been trained to interact with when given the opportunity.

I could hear my name being called out from somewhere. I stopped to take in the room, searching for the source of the voice. Unable to locate it, I proceeded on my path to sitting in solitude. I had almost made it when the voice rang out again, only this time, it was closer in proximity. I turned around, and there he was—Jackson Cooper.

It made perfect sense that he and his family would be here, but I had no way of knowing for sure, as my parents still had my phone, thus cutting off my communication with the outside world. I'd been hopeful that I would be able to lie low and not run into Jackson.

I gave the best smile I could manage along with a wave before turning back toward my destination. I knew that wouldn't be enough for him, but I needed a few seconds to clear my head and figure out what I could possibly say to him. My father had made it very clear that under no circumstances was he to find out that before today, he was a father-to-be.

I reached the back of the room and lowered myself into a chair as elegantly as I could. When Jackson caught up to me, he took a seat in the chair next to me and instantly reached for my hand. I wanted to pull away, but I let him take it. He brought it to his lips, giving it a gentle kiss.

"Hey. I've been so worried about you. You haven't been returning my texts for over a week. Is everything okay?"

No. Everything is the opposite of okay. Just this morning I was carrying your child, and now I'm not.

"Yeah, everything is fine. I lost my phone and just haven't gotten around to getting a new one yet."

"Oh thank God. I thought maybe I had done something to upset you," he said, running his hand over mine.

I looked deep into Jackson blue eyes—like two beautiful lagoons that I could've drowned in.

Jackson was the first man I had ever been intimate with. All throughout grade school, I was so focused on academics that I didn't even entertain the idea of dating. And most of the boys I met at functions like this were all the same. They didn't want a partner. They wanted a trophy. Jackson was the first guy to ever see me as more than Mayor Flores's daughter. He saw me as Anna and was genuinely interested in hearing *my* goals and *my* dreams for the future. He saw me as an *equal*.

The train tracks on the outskirts of town were our own little piece of heaven. We would just drive out there and sit in the car for hours and stare at the stars. Sometimes we sat in silence. Other times we would complain about our familial duties, but my favorite times were when we would share our deepest wants and dreams. We would imagine what our lives would look like if we were a part of any other family.

I shared things with him that I have never shared with anyone else, and never once did he reply with judgment or condescension. Our last trip there had been about a month ago, and that was the first time he'd told me he loved me. I hadn't realized it until that moment, but I loved him too. He leaned over and kissed me, and I reciprocated. I thought the whole fireworks scenario was just some dumb ploy that they used in romance movies, but the second his lips touched mine, warmth pulsed through my body in waves, like a tsunami crashing over a ship, taking it deep under the water. I wanted to keep sinking into him. Next thing I knew, we were lying in the backseat of his car, naked, with enough heat between us to start a raging fire.

He pulled away from me, and his eyes locked on to mine. "Are you sure you want to do this?" he asked in a soft voice.

During our many conversations, our sex lives had come up. I didn't have much to share, as mine had never existed up until that point, and he had only been with one other person. Hearing him be so cautious and caring in this moment only made me want to melt into him more.

"Yes. I'm sure," I said breathlessly.

We took another moment to stare into each other's eyes before our lips touched again, like two magnets that had no choice but to be attracted to one another, and well—you know the rest.

"What? No! You didn't do anything wrong!" I said, struggling to maintain eye contact with Jackson. Those eyes so easily transported me to that night and everything that had followed it over the past week.

"Okay, cool," he said, clearing his throat awkwardly.

Silence fell between us as I let my gaze wander around the room, taking in every detail in an attempt to figure out what to say next.

"This party is fun, right?" Jackson said.

"Oh yeah, can you not tell that I'm having a blast?"

We both broke out into laughter, and a jolt of pain sent my hand to my abdomen.

"Oh. Are you alright?" Jackson asked, leaning closer to me.

"I'm fine. Just—period cramps."

"Oh man, that's the worst," Jackson said as if he had any idea about what it felt like to have your body betray you on a monthly basis. "But at least that means you're not pregnant!"

If the cramps I was feeling hadn't been painful enough, those words felt like a knife being plunged into my heart. I tried to laugh it off, but my face refused to cooperate, and before I could let the first tear fall, I jumped from my chair and started toward the bathroom.

"Hey, did I say something?" Jackson asked, standing as well.

"I'm sorry. I'm just not feeling well. Excuse me."

I ran away from him and hid in the bathroom for the next hour, and by the time I returned to the party, he was gone.

From that moment on, Jackson and I were never the same. My body healed quickly, but my heart never quite bounced back. I couldn't look at him without being reminded of that day at Dr. Rollins's office. The one thing I had in this world that made me feel safe had been stripped from me by my father's lust for power. It became easier to be alone than to be with Jackson, and eventually, it got to the point where we only saw each other at social events. The lying got easier, and with each passing day, I built a wall between myself and Jackson Cooper. He never once pried, but instead would make sweet gestures or try to hold me. I so desperately longed for his touch to melt away the pain, but it was just easier for the both of us if I brushed him off—and so I did.

Eventually, he stopped trying to touch me, which broke my heart for him. All of the love between us faded like a flower plucked from the earth, slowly wilting until it was no longer recognizable.

Standing here now, and seeing him with Claire, I want to hate him, but I can't blame him. Jackson Cooper has always been filled with so much passion for life, and when I grew cold to him, it was only a matter of time until I froze him out completely. I wish I could forget all of the pain. I wish I could have stood up to my father and let him kick me to the curb. Jackson would have come to my rescue, and God only knows where we would be today.

He would have done anything to help us start a new life for our family, and I would have followed him absolutely anywhere. We wouldn't have to worry about impressing diplomats, wouldn't have to fake like we gave a shit about any of this. We would have lost everything, but as long as we had each other, we wouldn't need anything.

I wonder what he's feeling now that he knows the truth about what my father and his parents did to me. I wonder what he thinks of me for keeping this from him for so long. I would give everything to go back and change the story, but unfortunately, in life, there are no do-overs. All you can do is choose to let regret eat away at you until you are nothing more than a walking carcass. Or you can hope that you continue to learn and grow from the mistakes you made when you thought—no, you *believed*—you were doing the best you could at the time.

I run toward the car, my bare feet pounding against the

cold pavement. I hear the others calling out behind me, but I don't stop.

I *can't* stop.

I reach the car and melt into the driver's seat, breathless. My feet are throbbing as I pull my knees to my chest, burying my face into them. I think back to my mother. She was simply doing what she needed to do to survive my father. She never imagined being put in a situation where she would have to choose between her husband and her daughter.

I feel sympathy for her now.

When my back was against the wall, I made a choice and didn't care who got hurt in the aftermath.

It was me or Jackson—and I chose *me*.

It pains me more than anything to admit it, but I truly am my father's daughter.

CHAPTER
TWENTY-THREE
LOGAN

The tires of Jackson's truck screech to a halt in front of my dorm. Following the events of tonight, Julia ran after Anna and dropped herself into the passenger seat before Anna could drive away. I desperately wanted to follow after Julia, but with a topic as sensitive as this, I would have been of no use. Not to mention, Julia and Anna have a history, which is something I lack with all of my new "friends."

All of that to say, this is how I found myself stuck riding in the back seat of Jackson's truck. Claire drove while Jackson silently sobbed in the passenger seat, his shoulders occasionally jolting to stifle the scream that seemed like it could erupt any minute. Neither of them said a word on the drive over here, but every now and again I would look up from my phone to see Claire reaching over to place a hand on Jackson's leg—a futile attempt at comforting him. I spent the majority of the ride staring at my phone, watching the clock at the top of the screen. Every time the minute changed was one less minute I had left to spend in this cesspool of awkwardness.

I open my door, taking a moment to assess the large gap between my feet and the ground. I will never understand why someone would purposefully buy a truck that sits so high up from the ground. I'm sure there's some practical reason out there—like driving through a river, maybe—but judging by his clean-cut appearance, and the pristine exterior of his truck, Jackson isn't an "off-road" type of guy. I swivel my legs to the right before slowly sliding down the edge of my seat until my feet touch the ground. I feel like I should say something before shutting the door.

Have a good night! There is no way that's happening.

See you later! I kind of hope I don't, actually.

So are you two a couple now or— Nope. *Way* too soon.

I decide against speaking and just push the heavy door closed. The engine of the truck roars, reverberating off the brick walls of my dorm, and I watch as it drives out of view, disappearing into the night.

I turn and face the front entrance of my dorm—two large double doors with square frosted windows installed in each. A faint glow from the lobby lets me know that work study hours are over, and the junior who usually sits behind the front desk with his music blaring in his ears has gone home for the night.

I take a deep breath, the cold air filling my lungs, then release a sigh. After everything that has happened tonight, I should be utterly exhausted, but my mind is wide awake.

After the loss of my dad, it felt as though the weight of the world was suddenly placed on my shoulders. I was instantly promoted to the man of the house—whatever that means. I was tasked with writing the book that would end my father's twenty-year legacy, and on top of it all, I was still expected to go off to school the following fall.

Life stops for no one.

I would lie in bed, unable to sleep, my breathing strained by the crushing weight of my thoughts. I tried everything to quiet the voices, but the only thing that ever seemed to work was walking. I would leave the house at two in the morning and just walk around the neighborhood. The inside of each home would be dark, as if the house itself were resting with those inhabiting it. There were no sympathetic waves from neighbors, typically accompanied by empty conversation about the weather. There were no cars driving to and from work. There were no notifications, no unread emails on my phone. It was the one time of day where it felt as though time itself was frozen and I could sift through my thoughts without others offering input.

I turn from the double doors of my dorm, facing the grove just on the other side of the street with a sidewalk trail wrapping around the perimeter. I close my eyes to revel in the silence, breathing in the crisp air, before walking across the street and starting down the path.

I think of Anna. Since leaving the rec center, there have been no new messages in the group chat, which I guess is to be expected. Julia is busy comforting Anna, and Claire is busy comforting Jackson, which just leaves me on the outside. Every single one of them has had their darkest secrets forced into the light by User125249, and if their threats to expose us all rings true, then I am the final person on their hit list. I am a wounded swimmer stranded at sea. I know the shark is circling below, and it's only a matter of time until they strike, pulling me deep underwater, where no one can hear me scream.

A shiver forces its way down my spine, and I push the thoughts of impending doom away for now.

"No sense in worrying about things outside of your control," my dad would tell me. What I wouldn't give to have one more chat with him. One more time sitting across from each other at Rosie's Diner. He'd connect it all—the tunnel, the mannequin, the drugs, all of it.

Suddenly, every hair on the back of my neck rises to attention. Someone is watching me. I freeze, my eyes fixed on the trees that scatter the grove. Wind rattles the leaves overhead, and I focus, listening for any sound I can latch on to. A branch snaps to my right. Out of the corner of my eye, I catch a shadow shifting through the trees.

Time seems to stop. I know I should run, but in which direction? Every part of my being screams at me to flee from the shadow, to get as far as I can from the danger lurking in the distance. But I know that's not what my dad would do. He might have been terrified on the inside, but he never showed it. He would run toward danger, throwing caution to the wind.

Please watch over me, Dad.

Without another thought, I dart into the heart of the grove. My onlooker runs away, and I pick up my pace, relieved that whoever they are, they weren't planning on a fight.

Branches snap underfoot as the distance between us grows wider.

God, they're fast, I think to myself. My breaths are becoming more and more shallow. The cold air scorches my lungs as I force my body to keep going. The burn in my chest is nearly suffocating as each tree passes me by. I clear the last of them and come out on the other side of the grove, my eyes darting around for any sign of movement, but whoever it is is gone. Vanished into the night. My legs give out from under me, and I collapse onto the sidewalk until I'm able to catch my breath.

———

I walk the full perimeter of the grove twice before making my way back to the pavilion in the middle of the four dorms on campus. I think back to my first night here at Westview, when the pavilion was filled with mourning students holding candles and telling stories about the person Lexi Pruitt was. Little did I know, I would learn more than I ever wanted to about who she was in the weeks that would follow.

I reach the entrance, a large iron gate that arches across the top. I pull the gate open, the metal cold to the touch, and head for the angel. Maybe if I sit at the fountain long enough, she will share some of her wisdom and guidance.

The gate closes behind me with a clang that pings between the buildings. I wince, hoping that my carelessness hasn't disturbed anyone's sleep, and continue walking. After a few more steps, the fountain comes into view, stopping me dead in my tracks.

Sitting on the lip of the fountain is a single candlestick nestled into a silver base. The flame dances in the breeze that blows between the buildings, casting light and shadows across the damp stone. The candle itself is a deep red, the shade of blood, and the melted wax drips down the side as if from an open wound.

Have you ever known something to be true based solely on instinct? Like preparing for incoming rain despite the sky being cloudless. That gut feeling in the pit of your stomach that tells you something is wrong.

That feeling tells me that this candle was left here for me.

My heart pounds so hard, I fear at any moment my chest will crack open. The hair on the back of my neck stands upright and my eyes dart around, scanning the surrounding area for any onlookers watching from the cover of darkness. The silence I once welcomed almost feels deafening now. I steady my breath, listening intently for a shifting of leaves or a snapped branch, but there's nothing.

The rustling of papers draws my attention back to the fountain. Just under the silver base of the candle is a piece of paper, its edges fluttering with the breeze. I lift the candle, careful to not spill hot red wax down my arm. I lift the page from the damp stone. An email transcript fills the page, and I recognize the font as the one used by our mystery murderer. My brows knit together when I see the transcript is dated over a year ago. And not only that—it's addressed to Lexi Pruitt.

CHAPTER
TWENTY-FOUR

Hello Lexi,

As we all know, this campus was founded on the belief that excellence is created. It is a seed that is planted and tended to by countless hours of work and dedication toward your craft. With enough time and patience, that seed thrives and grows alongside us as we move through life.

This striving for excellence has been paved by many who came before us, and as time moves forward, we should never forget or take for granted the ones who embodied this culture we cultivate here at Westview.

We would like to start a series that honors those who are gone but not forgotten, and we would like to start with someone who we all agree truly embodied this excellence while he was with us—the late Jeff Pruitt.

The loss of one of this nation's best lawyers was unprecedented and felt in homes from coast to coast. Throughout his career, he helped many families in need and was a real advocate for the underdogs. It was this mission to expose the shortcomings of the justice system in an attempt to fight for marginalized communities that really earned him his claim to fame.

He later began to take on heavy hitters in the political world, and he claimed to be America's "guy on the inside." Many rallied behind him in this mission and believed he would be the true voice of the people.

While many revered Jeff, he was, in fact, only human, and it did not take long before he got a taste of the plague that eventually poisoned his mind.

Now, as mentioned before, Jeff began to take on more wealthy clients, and we all know that where there is wealth, there is power. Jeff realized this and used the power of his new clients to—shall we say—persuade witnesses before taking the stand. He knew that keeping his winning streak would expedite his rise to the top, and he was willing to do whatever it took to make sure he won, even if it meant providing an alleged eyewitness to testify and sway the jury in his direction.

That's right. Jeff Pruitt, the man who was destined to advocate for the underdog, who took people's desire for a better life and used it to his advantage. Neighbors were sentencing each other to life in prison like a modern-day Salem, and all it took was a promise for a better life. Funny how people are so quick to turn on each other when their backs are against the wall and there's a paycheck dangling in front of their noses like a carrot.

Is this the kind of man we would like to remain part of our legacy here at Westview? Jeff Pruitt was a liar, a cheat, and a menace to those who work hard every day just to barely scrape by. I believe we speak for the community when we say that this man does not embody the excellence that is expected of a Westview alumnus, and, while we don't believe that his legacy should be erased from our hallowed halls, we should remember this man and his grievous actions, and strive to be better.

Our condolences—and disappointment,
  —The Ghost Writers

CHAPTER
TWENTY-FIVE
LOGAN

I scan the page in my hand, soaking in every detail it has to offer. The text and formatting all resemble the articles from User125249—the only difference being the signature at the bottom.

According to this, this article was written by the Ghost Writers, but why would they want to go after one of their own? It doesn't make sense.

I fold the paper into a small rectangle and shove it deep into my jacket pocket before lifting my hands to rub my eyes. Exhaustion settles over my body as the questions begin to pile on top of one another. It will be at least a few days until I'm able to ask the others about this, so I decide it's best to not worry about it now.

I scan the pavilion once more for any sign of movement. The windows of the surrounding buildings are all dark, and I push away the thought that someone could be watching me from their perch, reveling in my torment.

I'm starting back toward the front entrance of my dorm when a light catches the corner of my eye. I look up to the second-story window, to my room set aglow by the overhead light.

That's strange. I could have sworn that I turned the lights off before Anna picked me up, but with everything going on as of late, leaving the light on is the least of my worries. The window to my room stands out like a beacon, calling me to rest. Through the open window, I can see— Wait. My window is *open*.

My heart drops as I think back to that first night in my dorm and the disappointment that I felt when I discovered it was sealed shut. I know for a fact that I haven't tampered with the window, which leaves only one possibility—someone has been in my room between the time Anna picked me up and now. I shift and lean from side to side, scanning the room through the window and listening for any sign that they're still inside.

I start toward the main entrance, the pace of my steps increasing until I'm at a full jog. I yank the doors open and run through the empty lobby, my heart pounding as I turn each corner. Darting into the stairwell, I check above me for anyone who might still be trying to make their escape, but no one else is here. Upon reaching the second floor, I take a moment to steady my breath before treading down the silent hallway. I press my ear against the thick door, listening for anything that could be awaiting me on the other side.

Breathe in. Breathe out. The mantra repeats. I steady my breath, blocking out the world around me like I'm a horse fitted with blinders. I slide my key into the lock as quietly as possible. If someone is on the other side of this door, I don't want them to know I'm coming. But if they've been watching me since I entered the pavilion, they could be right there, prepared to attack.

Without giving it another thought, I turn the key in the lock and barge into the empty room, my fists bared.

My eyes take in the room at lightning speed. Lucky for me, my dorm room is quaint, and the spaces large enough for someone to hide are few and far between. I first check behind the door.

Clear.

I squat down and look underneath my bed to see a couple of unpacked boxes covered in dust.

Clear.

The only other option is the bathroom to my left, but in the large mirror that covers the wall, I can see the reflection of the shower curtain gathered to one side. I step inside and check behind the bathroom door and let out a sigh of relief when I see that it's vacant.

Clear.

Stepping back into my bedroom, I take inventory, looking for anything that could be missing or moved around. Other than the draft gliding in through the open window, everything seems to be exactly where I left it. I push down on the window pane until it slides into place with a *thunk,* ensuring the two locks are fastened into place before plopping onto the bed with a crumpling sound.

I feel like the princess with the pea as I sink into my bed. I can't quite put my finger on it, but something is off. And what was that sound? I stand from the bed and pull the covers back and locate the source.

A sealed envelope the size of a full sheet of paper has been placed on the bed with the words *OPEN ME* written in blood-red ink. I lift the envelope with shaky hands, terrified of the contents. The seal rips, and I pull out what looks to be a picture. The yellow tape pictured in the bottom corner tells me that this is a picture taken from a crime scene. There's a car I don't recognize, crumpled, gleaming in the red and blue lights.

Is this the car that Lexi was in when she died? Why would the person who broke into my room want me to see this?

In the top right corner of the picture is another car in a similar state as what I assume is Lexi's car, only this one looks familiar. I can't quite place my finger on it—until I notice the license plate hanging from the back bumper.

Every square inch of my body goes cold, like I'm trapped in a block of ice with no hope of escape. I rub my eyes, certain I must have seen it wrong, but when I open them again, the picture is the same. Every hope of getting sleep tonight is out the window. I fold the picture and place it in the pocket with the article I found in the pavilion.

I open my phone to order the first available cab. I should wait until morning to start looking for answers, but now that I know what I know, that is no longer an option. Each step closer to the main exit feels like a dream sequence, like I am the helpless victim running in the woods with the killer right on my tail. Reality blurs with fiction, and I don't know who to trust anymore. I have questions that demand answers, and there's only one person who knows the truth.

The cab pulls up just outside the main entrance to my dorm. I'm so focused on finding the truth that I don't even give a second thought before getting in. As the car lurches forward, I send a text to announce my arrival in the next hour or so.

It's time to do the one thing I have been avoiding since I was dropped off here at Westview.

I need to pay my mother a visit.

CHAPTER
TWENTY-SIX
LOGAN

I will the car toward its destination, trying to piece together the fragmented shards of my memory. There must be some sort of explanation for the second crumpled car present at the scene of my accident. The night is a blur.

When I woke up in the hospital, my mom made it seem like I just lost control of the car. There were heavy rains, the road was slick, and it was just some sort of freak accident. I play the conversation over in my head. Never once did she mention another car on the scene.

Why would she hide that from me?

I try to come to grips with the fact that my mother has been lying to me for over a year, and it feels as though my reality is shattering, pointed shards chipping away to reveal the truth. How was there no story on this? How has my name eluded the media surrounding Lexi's death?

My mother can't lie to me anymore. There's a picture in my pocket that proves I was there the night Lexi died.

I check my phone as the cab pulls up to my family

home. I'm surprised to see that my mother hasn't texted me back, but the porch light is on, so I know she's expecting me.

I fumble with my keys as I make my way to the front door. Inside, I'm immediately greeted by Sadie, my mom's goldendoodle, who welcomes me with licks and excess barking. It isn't long before my mother comes out of her room to investigate, and the moment she catches sight of me, she runs to hold me in her arms.

It's been months since I've had my mother wrap me up like this, and I realize just how much I need it. As I hug her in return, I feel the emotions of the last couple months melt into tears streaming down my face. She holds me tighter, my sobs growing more and more uncontrollable. We stay like that until my tears are exhausted.

"What are you doing here, sweetie?" my mom asks. We pull away from each other, but she keeps me at arm's length, making sure not to let go. I stare for a moment, searching for my words

"We need to talk about the accident," I say, my voice tight.

She presses her lips together, and the look in her eyes tells me that she knew this day would come—or, perhaps, hoped that it never would.

"Go take a seat in the living room," she says. "I'll make us some tea."

I do as I'm told. In the living room, I look around at the moody decor as memories flash over me. Sitting and watching old movies as a family, sandwiched on the couch between my mom and dad. Waking up early on a Saturday to turn on the radio and listen to my dad's interview about his new book. The day we brought Sadie home and I slept on the living room floor with her so she wouldn't be afraid. These memories are all I have left of my family before it all fell apart.

My mom comes into the living room, balancing two cups of tea, her steps muted by the fuzzy slippers on her feet. I take the tea from her hand, and she takes her place in the chair to my right. She's silent at first, taking a sip of her tea before she finally speaks.

"What do you want to know?" she asks in a low tone.

That's a loaded question. There are so many things I want to know. Where could I possibly begin?

"The truth," I start. "What really happened that night? Was there someone else involved in the accident?"

My mom takes a moment before answering, the words heavy in her throat.

"Yes."

A part of me knew what she would say, but there was another part of me that still hoped it wasn't true.

"Why didn't you tell me?" New tears form in my eyes.

"I wanted to protect you. You were my baby, and you weren't the same after your father—" The last of the sentence sticks in her throat. "I was worried about you. You had grown so distant; you weren't sleeping, you wouldn't talk to me. I didn't know what was going on in your head. And then—that night when I woke up and you were gone, I thought you had—" She shudders at the words she can't bring herself to say. "Well, you know. And if I added this to your plate—"

"So *that's* why you didn't tell me about Lexi? You thought I would try to kill myself?"

"Lexi?" she asks, ignoring the second half of my question. "Who's Lexi?"

"The girl who was in the other car."

"I never asked her name. When I got to the scene,

Officer Scott informed me that the girl had been unconscious behind the wheel long before you drove up there. You were just in the wrong place at the wrong time. It wasn't your fault, so I didn't see a problem in keeping it from you."

I want to scream. If only she knew the hell I've been through back at school. Instead, I force my face into my hands, taking deep breaths to keep a calm tone.

"I just wish you would have told me, Mom. Because now—" I stop myself before I can finish.

"Now what?" My mother leans into me with her signature one eyebrow raised.

I sit in silence, contemplating what I should tell her, which only makes her more persistent to hear everything. So, I tell her everything.

"Okay, wait, so how did this person know about the car crash?" my mother asks when I'm finished, like we're two detectives working on the same case.

"I don't know, Mom. That's why we've been trying to figure out what happened that night. Whoever they were, they were able to get a hold of a picture from the night of the accident."

"A picture? But the police didn't take—"

"I don't know, Mom. But obviously *someone* took a picture. Here, let me show you."

I pull the folded-up photo from my pocket, gently smoothing out the creases before handing it out to her. My phone lights up on the coffee table, grabbing her attention.

"Oh my gosh, your little group of friends is so cute," she says looking at my Lock Screen—the selfie Claire took after I was inducted into the Ghost Writers Club. "When can I meet them?"

I drop the picture onto the table and try to snatch my

phone from her, but before I can reach it, she swipes it farther away, moving the screen closer to her face.

"Mom. Please give me back my phone. This is serious."

"Ah! I didn't know that nice girl went to your school!"

I look at my mother, perplexed. I've hardly spoken to my mom since the school year started, so I know for a fact that she shouldn't know anyone in that picture.

"What are you talking about, Mom? You've never met any of those people."

"Yes, I have. I might not be good with names, Logan, but I can remember a face. I'll never forget her face, really, since she was the only one who came to visit you in the hospital."

The hospital? I think back to the gift on the windowsill. My mom told me someone dropped it off, and I assumed it was Emily. But thinking back, my mom never confirmed that it was actually her. Why would any of them have visited me if they didn't know who I was? They couldn't know what room I was in—unless they followed me from the scene of the accident.

"Mom," I say, sliding my phone in her direction. "Can you point to the person you met at the hospital?"

She pauses, taking in the picture briefly before placing her finger on the phone. When my eyes meet the face of the person who has been tormenting us for weeks, my heart drops to the floor.

I stand from the couch and head straight for the door. I look at the keys hanging from the hook on the wall, grabbing them before I can realize what I'm doing.

"Honey, shouldn't you wait until morning to head back? It's late, and you know you haven't driven since—"

"Mom, I love you, but I need you to trust me."

Before she can protest, I open the door and step out of

my house for what I hope is not the final time. I'm halfway down the driveway when my mother's voice calls from the front of the house.

"Logan!"

I look to see her standing in the doorway, tears glowing in the moonlight.

"*Please* be safe. I can't lose you again."

"You won't. I love you, Mom."

She mouths the words back to me, her voice unable to escape her throat.

I stare at her a moment longer before lowering myself into the car. I open my phone to a notification from User125249.

ROSIE'S DINER. 2AM. BE THERE OR THE ARTICLES GO LIVE. SEE YOU SOON :)

I turn the key in the ignition, saying a little prayer that driving a car is like riding a bike. You never really forget how to do it.

I close my eyes for a moment, hoping that wherever my dad is, he is proud of his son.

Breathe in. Breathe out.

Before I can overthink it, I throw the car into gear. I press on the gas as the car slowly comes up to speed, and I'm on my way to finally meet User125249.

CHAPTER
TWENTY-SEVEN
LEXI

THE NIGHT OF THE ACCIDENT

t's always fun exposing the truth—until it's yours.

We all have secrets. Some of us are just better at keeping them buried than others.

I can hear the sound of my stepfather shouting, which is usually just background noise to me at this point. If he isn't shouting at my mother to bring him a beer, he's berating her for attracting too much attention from other men. I always wonder how my mom ended up with someone like him. My father dying was the first time that I ever saw my mom break down, and even in her shattered state, she was beautiful. She could have her pick of any eligible bachelor, but somehow she ended up with Sean fucking Reynolds.

Sean was great at first. He would take us to nice dinners as a family, he would buy my mother extravagant bouquets of flowers, and some days, he would bring home presents for her and me. Sean was the first person to make my mom truly happy after my father died, but it wasn't long after their wedding day that the facade began to crack. Turns out he was a nobody from nowhere and was only into my mom because of who my dad was. More importantly, the money he left behind.

My dad was the number-one lawyer on the West Coast, and he made a killing in the courtroom. I think it was his pursuit of the truth and his ability to catch people in a lie that made me want to use my writing for something good. I wanted to bring the truth out of people in the same way my father did.

I saw through Sean the moment I met him. I tried to convince my mom to stop seeing him, but in her vulnerable state, she was easily whisked into his recipe for disaster that became our life. Sean had wormed his way into the family and managed to convince my mother to forego a prenup, so the second they both signed on the dotted line, he held claim to at least half of the money that was left behind to her.

My mom tried to leave him, but his threats to ruin her life and leave her with nothing forced her to stay. She was stuck.

I am stuck.

Honestly, who knows where I would be if not for Julia? She has been the one person—the only person—to provide me with any inkling of hope for a better life.

From the moment I met her, I thought she was the most beautiful girl in the world. I could see us growing old together. Our relationship blossomed quickly, and neither of us knew we were in love until it was too late. It happened slowly, right under our noses. She became my calm in the middle of the shit storm I was forced to call home. We would meet up for coffee or a chocolate malt shake at Rosie's Diner and talk about anything and everything.

We would talk on the phone all night long and hate ourselves the next morning and then do it all over again. Julia seemed to always fall asleep before I did, and I sometimes referred to her as "my old lady."

I have always been a night owl. I seemed to do my best writing when the world around me was asleep and the magic the stars seemed to share was mine for the taking. I wanted to make a name for myself with my writing, and Julia was the first person I ever met whose abilities matched the caliber of my own. Sometimes she would come over and we would sneak up to the rooftop of my apartment building. We would sit and share our stories with each other, the night sky a witness to our blossoming love.

Sometimes, in moments like this, when Sean is yelling one thing or another, I close my eyes. I'm transported to the rooftop, and I smile.

I think back to a few weeks ago. Julia and I were sharing our plans for our future, and we shared the same priority—leaving this town.

"Run away with me," she said, her eyes glistening in the moonlight. We had joked about running away together many times, but this time, I could tell that she meant it. All I could do was look at her. Of course I wanted to run away with her, but there was so much to think about. She was the hopeless romantic, and I was the analytical one. Opposites attract, I guess.

"I would love to," I started, "but—"

With that one three-letter word, her smile vanished as fast as it appeared.

"What if we waited until graduation? I just think we

need to take the time to figure out getting a new apartment and find work before we leave. And then there's my mom."

"You don't want to leave her alone with Sean."

"Yeah," I said, grimacing at the mention of his name.

Julia and I both share a strong distaste for Sean. How could she not after all the venting I've done to her about how horrible and vile of a human he is to my mother and me? I see all of the things he does to her with me in the house, and I can't bear the thought of what he might do when they are alone.

I reached out to grab Julia's hand.

"Please understand, Julia. I would leave with you today if he weren't in the picture."

At that moment, I couldn't tell if I felt sadness toward my mother, or anger toward her blissful ignorance that landed us in this position. I would have left a long time ago had it not been for her hasty decision to find a man to fill the void that my father left behind.

I have become a prisoner to her choices and put my life on hold to protect the woman who raised me. I feel like I owe her my life, even if that life doesn't include Julia.

The voices behind the door let me know that it's time for bed. I stretch across my bed, and I'm about to close my laptop when it chimes with a notification. I lift the screen to see that I have received a direct message from the Ghost Writers webpage. I click on the notification, prompting an article to fill the screen—more specifically, an article with my father's name on it.

CHAPTER
TWENTY-EIGHT
LEXI

THE NIGHT OF THE ACCIDENT

Rage.

I stare at the article. My cheeks feel so hot that my tears evaporate before making it to my chin. I understand Anna being pissed off about me wanting to publish the article about her father, but to go after someone who's no longer here to defend themselves? That is a new low.

I slam my laptop closed and stare at the door to my room. The house is eerily still as I stew in my anger.

I think of my dad. I don't want to believe that any of this is true, and the worst part about it is, I will *never* know the truth.

I wish more than anything I could talk to him right now. He knew the answers to all of my questions, even though he would answer them like he was convincing a jury to vote in his favor. I have always thought of my dad as the truth crusader, and after he passed, I decided to take on that role in his honor. If this article is accurate, then I'm certain that truth doesn't exist in this world. It can't. There is only reality—and billions of people who consider their *perception* of reality the truth.

I see now that the Ghost Writers are no different. They each have their own version of reality and believe it to be their truth, and they will do whatever it takes to protect it. Julia is different, though. I think about how strong she is after everything she went through in her family. She is the only person in the world who understands how it feels to be trapped in a mess you didn't make, which is why we can't wait to get out of this town and start our own story. I close my eyes and imagine us on a porch somewhere, reading our books and watching the sun fade into night. We can go anywhere and be anything. We can finally be free.

I stand from the bed and grab my backpack from the chair in the corner of my room. I shove my laptop in along with a couple of wads of clothes from the piles scattered along the floor.

I am leaving.

I am taking Julia, and we are going to drive into our freedom. Thunder shakes the house, and I peek outside to see the rain falling in slanted sheets. It feels as though Mother Nature has offered me a gift—a symphony of racket to flee in undetected.

I finish packing my bag and head for the door, opening it slowly to peek out into the darkness. I tiptoe through the living room, ensuring that each step makes minimal noise. On my way through the kitchen, I take Sean's keys from the counter, but I stop when I reach the front door. I turn back, facing the living room to listen for movement on the second floor, but there's nothing but silence accompanied by the occasional rumble of thunder.

I walk out of the house, careful to close the door softly. When the latch snaps into place, I run down the driveway, using my bag as a shield from the heavy rain, down to the street where Sean's car is parked. I pull on the driver's-side door, and I'm caught off guard when it opens. This car is Sean's baby. Why would be so careless as to leave it unlocked? My best guess is that Sean and my mom's argument started in the car and continued all the way into the house. Perhaps in the heat of the moment, he forgot? At this point, it really doesn't matter.

I lower myself into the driver's seat and pull out my phone. I bring up Julia's name and quickly type a message.

> I'm taking Sean's car and I'm coming to pick you up. Pack a bag and I'll be at your place in about ten minutes.

> I love you so much, Julia.

I drive down the winding roads as the windshield wipers work vigorously to clear the water obstructing my view. I know these roads by heart and can basically drive them in my sleep. The windows begin to fog up, and I quickly look at the dashboard, trying to keep one eye on the road. I turn the knob for the air, and, in an instant, the car is filled with a cloud of fine powder collecting around my face and eyes. I slam on the brakes, sliding into the other lane before finally coming to a halt. I break into a coughing fit and can feel my chest tighten up. I roll down the window to air out the car. Rainwater pours into the car as I focus on getting my breathing under control.

I reach for my phone to call for help and notice a notification from Julia. My vision is shrouded in darkness, closing farther in with each strained breath. Before I open the message, a bright light comes from around the bend in the road, bound directly for me.

With my last bout of consciousness, I forward the article, hitting send and forcing my eyes closed to block out the beams. My body feels like it's floating, like I am submerged underwater, sinking farther and farther below the surface.

And then—it's over.

I sit in the intersection, waiting for the light to turn green. From here, I can see my destination just across the street: Rosie's Diner, looking like a weathered relic that could topple over with the slightest gust of wind. I scan the dark parking lot and spot Jackson's car.

The light turns green, and I slowly roll up to the diner, making sure to turn off my headlights before entering the parking lot. I pull my car up next to Jackson's truck and kill the engine. I take a moment to absorb the dilapidated structure before me. Shingles hang from the roof, and some patches are missing entirely. The walls are layered with dirt and graffiti, peeking out from under the dead vines. The windows are hazy with dust and grime, but I can see broken blinds hanging inside. I look through the gaps, searching for any sign of life on the other side, but all I find is darkness. Everything inside me screams to start the car and go home to my mother, but I couldn't live with myself if something happens to the others and I'm the final nail in

Lexi's coffin. I know that once I step inside, there's a chance I won't walk out.

I take a few deep breaths, trying to calm my racing heart, but the uncertainty of what awaits me in the diner only heightens my anxiety. I close my eyes, take one last deep breath, and finally open the car door, making my way up the small wooden stairs to Rosie's. The door has a hole where the knob should be, and with a light push, it creaks open, announcing my arrival.

Aromas of rotted wood and gasoline singe my nostrils, and I cup my hands around my mouth and nose like a barrier. As my eyes adjust, the state of the diner comes into focus. Once bustling with life and vibrant with color, the inside of Rosie's now resembles something you'd see in the apocalypse. Everything as it was, only preserved in layers of dust and grime. The red stools surrounding the bar stand weary, helplessly hoping to welcome one more guest.

I tense when I see a silhouette sitting in a booth at the far end of the diner. My eyes are fixed on the back of their head, trying to detect the rise and fall of their breath.

"Hello," I call out. "A-are you okay?"

No response.

I hold my breath with each creaking step, mentally preparing for the worst. Halfway across the diner, the table comes into view, and I see the word *SIT* scrawled across the table in red paint. Or is it blood? Oh my God. What if the person sitting at this table right now is dead? My stomach turns, and I feel like I'm going to be sick. I reach out a shaking hand, nearly touching their shoulder, when a voice rings out from behind me.

"Logan! Over here!" Claire calls out. I nearly jump out

of my skin and quickly turn to see Jackson, Anna, and Claire standing in the doorway.

"Do you know what the fuck is going on?" Jackson asks as I rush over to meet them. I don't know the answer to his question, but I do know that we need to get out of here as soon as possible.

"I don't have time to explain," I say, breathless. "We have to get out of —"

"Who is that?" Claire asks, walking toward the silhouette seated at the table. I try to stop her from seeing what I was too afraid to confirm on my own, but I'm too late. Her bloodcurdling scream tells me everything I need to know.

"Oh my God! It's Benson!" She clasps her hands around her mouth. "He's dead!"

The three of us run over, taking in the horrific sight. Benson sits propped like a puppet, his pale, lifeless skin set aglow by moonlight. His gray shirt hangs from his body, and a dark red stain covers his chest.

I think back to the mannequin from the library. The way the knife jutted out of its chest. It would appear Benson suffered the same fate, and whoever killed him wanted us or the police to know exactly how his life came to an end.

A loud commotion from the kitchen severs my attention, and I retreat until I feel the edge of the table pressing into my back. Anna jumps at the noise, knocking into Benson's body and sending him toppling to the ground. In his current state, I'm sure he doesn't mind.

I stare into the darkness, looking for any shift in the shadows.

"Julia? Is that you?" Claire calls out, her voice shaky. "We're in here—at the table."

A muffled groan sounds from the abyss beyond the

door, growing closer by the second. My mouth falls open when a bloodied hand reaches across the doorframe, illuminated by the moonlight filtering through the broken windows.

"Holy shit!" Jackson shouts, moving in front of Anna like a shield. With everything I know about Anna and the things she went through, she is the strongest of us all. I half expect her to push him out of the way, but she lets Jackson stay where he is.

I watch in horror as the hand lurches forward, pulling the rest of the body along the checkered floor. This continues until they collapse, their face now exposed in the dim light.

"Is that—Sean?" Anna asks over Jackson's shoulder, panic rising in her voice.

The man before us lies on the floor, lifeless. I don't know what has happened to him since he went missing, but it for sure hasn't been pleasant, as evidenced by the bruises and open wounds on his face and arms.

"Fuck this. I'm getting out of here," Jackson says, taking Anna's hand in his and moving toward the door. Anna pulls her hand from his grip, and he turns to her in disbelief.

"What are you doing? We need to go."

"And do what, Jackson? Where can we go? If those stories about us get out, we have no future to run to!"

"I don't care about those articles! I'll face the consequences. It's a hell of a lot better than dying here."

Jackson reaches for her hand again, but she pulls it out of reach. He stands for a moment, a pleading look in his eyes. "Come with me, Anna. *Please!*"

Anna remains silent, telling Jackson everything he needs to hear. He starts for the door, his boots thudding against the floor. He's about to place his hand against the door when it swings open on its own, freezing him in his tracks. Julia steps in, and my eyes widen.

"Oh thank God, Julia. We have to call your dad. Benson is dead, and there's a guy here, and he's hurt really bad," Jackson explains, trying to move around Julia, who blocks the entrance.

"Did you not hear what I just said? There's a guy hurt, and we're all in danger! We have to get—"

"Sit down, Jackson," Julia says in an eerily low tone.

"Julia . . . what are you doing?" Jackson says, looking at the gun in Julia's hand, now pressing against his chest.

Julia jolts her hand up, firing a round into the air with a deafening bang, sending dust and debris swirling around us. Jackson falls to the floor, shaking like a small dog, and as the dust settles, I see Julia is aiming the gun at his face.

"I said, sit."

Jackson scoots backward on the floor away from her. He stands and raises his hands to eye level, shuffling back to his seat and keeping his eyes fixed on the gun.

"You too, Logan."

I freeze, caught in a trance, the scene playing out before me a nightmare I can't wake up from. I turn to see Claire's wide, terrified eyes begging me to comply. My gaze flits back to Julia as I slowly lower myself into my seat.

"Why are you doing this, Julia?" Anna asks through gritted teeth.

"Don't worry, Anna. We'll get there. I've been planning this night for a long time, and I don't want to rush it."

Sean's body twitches as he writhes on the filthy floor, groaning through the duct tape covering his mouth. He presses his blood-crusted hands against the ground, attempting to lift himself, but he collapses again, the fight fading from his bones.

"Don't worry, Sean. It will all be over soon," she says, like he's a harmless pet.

Julia steps over to the high-top bar, the gun in her hand fixed on us as she rests her free elbow on the splintered counter.

"Now that the cat is out of the bag, I think it's time for a little story."

CHAPTER
THIRTY
JULIA

was there the night Lexi died.

The second I saw her text, I pulled up her location on my phone, tapping the screen to populate directions. I ran down the stairs, an electric panic coursing through every nerve, burning me from the inside out.

I did what I could to calm my breathing as I pulled my car off the side of the road and sped toward the location marked on screen.

The road curved, bending around mountains and hills, and as I came around the final bend, I could feel my heart shattering in my chest, the broken shards threatening to rip me apart. I was too late.

I recognized the crumpled car as Lexi's. As quickly as I could, I pulled the car off the side of the road.

"Lexi!" The sound ripped from my throat as I ran from my car across the dark street.

Please be okay. Please be okay. The thought repeated in my mind on a loop.

I reached through the broken window, lifting Lexi's limp head as tears streamed down my face.

"Come on, Lexi. Wake up," I begged, rubbing my fingers across her cheeks made rosy by the cold. "Please, baby. Wake up. I did this for us! This wasn't meant for you. Please wake up."

It felt as though the air had been sucked from my lungs. Part of me hoped the air would never return. How could I grow old without my person by my side?

I was the one who stole Claire's inhaler.

I was the one who emptied the contents into the air vents in an attempt to get rid of Sean.

If I had just been more patient, Sean would have probably drank himself to death.

He would be gone, Lexi would be alive, and all of this would just be a bad dream. I tried to stop her, sending her a text to warn her about what I had done, but I was too late.

This is all my fault.

The thought taunted me, laughed at me. The mocking grew louder until the world around me became static.

"Help!" a voice called out.

I lifted my head, thinking I must have lost my mind, but then the voice called out again.

"Is anyone there? I'm trapped and I need help!"

I stood from the road, looking for the source of the voice. Off the side of the road, concealed in shadows, was another car. I was so focused on getting to Lexi that I hadn't even noticed.

As I approached, I saw four tires where the top of the car should have been. They'd flipped.

"Hello! I'm here!" they called out like an animal begging to be released from their cage.

"I'm here! I'm going to call for help right now."

I lifted my phone to call for help, but I saw a notification from Lexi. When the message opened, I saw a group of letters and symbols typed and underlined in blue font. It was a link.

I tapped the screen and saw an article written by the Ghost Writers. Lexi's dad was the subject. I hadn't written any of this. I would never have done anything to hurt Lexi. She had to know that I had no part in this article.

Was this why she changed her mind so quickly about running away with me?

"This is all *their* fault." The words escaped my lips.

If they had just kept their stupid mouths shut, Lexi would still have been at home, and Sean would have been dead within the week. We could have left town, and bought some land, and just existed together until the end of our days. They took everything away from me.

My eyes lifted to the overturned car that placed the final nail in Lexi's coffin.

"No. *You* took everything from me."

I stood there a moment, watching him writhe in place to break free from his shackles. Why should he be the one to survive and not Lexi? It just wasn't fair. He had to pay for what he did. So, I left him there to die. He screamed for me to help him, crying out like a child to his mother. Pathetic.

I got into my car and drove away, leaving my love behind for the final time.

A few days later, I overheard my dad talking with another officer, which was when I discovered that Logan had managed to survive. According to the report, he was trapped in his car for at least a few hours before the first responders got to him. Maybe he wasn't as pathetic as I thought, but either way, it was high time I paid him a visit. When my dad wasn't looking, I snuck into his office and took a peek at the report.

With his name etched into my memory, I made my way to the hospital to find him. I stood in the open doorway to his room and saw a woman sitting in a chair in the corner, her face buried deep into her hands.

"Excuse me," I whispered, prompting the woman to lift her gaze in my direction. "I heard about Logan and—"

"Oh my goodness, are you one of his friends? I didn't think Logan had any friends."

Machinery whirred and beeped around the room, each piece tethered to Logan's life. Every beep of the heart monitor was one more heartbeat that he didn't deserve. Had his mother not been there, I would have already had a pillow placed firmly over his pathetic face.

She took the gift from my hands and placed it on the windowsill before taking her place in her seat.

"You're welcome to stay a while if you like. Though the doctors think it'll be a day or two until he's coherent."

"That's okay. I just wanted to stop by and wish him well," I said with the fakest smile I could muster.

Those were my final words to that annoying woman, and imagine my shock when the next year, Logan, the man who killed Lexi, was the talk of campus. Every administrator was buzzing with the news that Leonard Clark's legacy would grace the halls of Westview once again.

I had hoped that his father's curious nature had been passed down to him when I mentioned the Ghost Writers Club. He took the bait without hesitation. I had him exactly where I wanted him, and it was time for the plan to be set in motion.

Benson, being the loser he was, was so quick to jump at

the opportunity to get back at Anna and Claire for embarrassing him in front of the entire school. I would write and send Benson the articles, and tell him when to send them to the group. He thought all of this was a harmless prank—until it wasn't.

You should have seen the look on his face when I told him I needed blood from him. He told me I was crazy and that I was taking things too far, but when it comes to love, there is no such thing as too far. Since he wouldn't give me his blood willingly, I took it by force, plunging a knife into his chest and watching as shock melted into fear and he took his final breath.

Sean, on the other hand, took a bit more strategy. Lexi had told me all the time about how he would step out on his marriage with her mom. I used that to my advantage and created a dating profile, using a picture of a woman's chest I found on Google as the profile picture.

In less than a week, Sean Reynolds was sending me messages, begging to take me out on a date. When I finally agreed, he suggested something discreet, which of course I didn't mind. The more discreet the better. He played right into my hand, thinking he would have some fun and get away with it. Instead, he ended the night with a brick over his head. I bound him and managed to get him into the trunk.

Once he had been properly stored, I drove here, to the place where everything began—Rosie's Diner. It was here that I kept him until all the pawns were in place.

Each and every one of the Ghost Writers, including me, deserves to die.

Everyone in this dark, decrepit diner had a part in taking Lexi from this earth, and it's time for us to pay for our sins.

CHAPTER
THIRTY-ONE
LOGAN

"What are you going to do to us?" Jackson asks.

"I am going to bring justice for Lexi. An eye for an eye. A life for a life."

Claire, who up to this point has managed to remain somewhat composed, now sobs loudly. She rocks in her seat, repeating, "I'm so sorry, Lexi" on a loop like a record skipping, prompting a laugh from Julia.

"Sorry? Do you really think being sorry will do you any good?" Julia asks the room. "Do you think it will do *any* of us any good? We killed her, and the only way to make it right is to give our lives in return."

"So you're just going to shoot us and leave us for dead? Someone is bound to come looking for us." Anna says, trying to reason with her.

With her free hand, Julia reaches into her pocket, revealing a single match—the final piece of her plan now out on display.

"Not if there isn't a place for them to look."

My heart pounds, and I begin to feel light-headed. Julia wants to set Rosie's Diner ablaze with all of us trapped inside—our own personal hell to repent for our mistakes. My first thought goes to my mom, standing in the driveway and pleading for me to return home in one piece.

I wish so badly I could have kept that promise to her, but I hope in the end, she will be proud of my courage. All I ever wanted was to prove to her that I could stand on my own two feet following my accident. I was so wrapped up in gaining my independence that I neglected her feelings along the way. She was hurting too. She lost someone too. Tears spring to my eyes at the thought that she will never get the apology she deserves.

Suddenly, Jackson leaps from the table, charging full speed at Julia. "I can't let you do this!"

A loud bang sends Jackson crumbling to the floor, clutching his arm and screaming out in pain.

Holy shit. She shot him. She really shot him.

"No!" Anna cries out, nearly falling out of the booth in her attempt to aid Jackson.

"Sit down!" Julia shouts.

A storm of chaos and grief swirls behind her darkened eyes as she aims the gun in Anna's direction. Anna freezes, crying out for mercy with her hands raised before quickly returning to her seat.

"I don't want to shoot you!" Julia starts, the gun in her hand visibly shaking. "Just do as I say and it will all be over soon."

A flashing light floods through the broken windows, casting jagged shadows of red and blue over everything in sight.

A moment later, the door to the diner flings open with a loud thud, and Officer Scott materializes in the entryway with his gun drawn. He freezes in place, looking down the sight of his gun at his own flesh and blood.

"Julia—sweetie, you don't have to do this."

"Lexi dying is all our fault, and we have to pay for what we did to her."

"Julia—" Officer Scott's voice cracks. "*Please* don't do this. We can get through this together—you, me, and Mom."

Julia scoffs. "What can Mom possibly do? You have *ruined* her and treated her like shit! And all she ever did was love you!"

"I have made some mistakes—just like you have, sweetie. That doesn't mean anyone else needs to die."

"I'm sure Mom would be better off if you were dead. Maybe I should do her a favor while I'm at it," Julia says, turning her focus to the match in her hand.

"Julia, don't! I don't want to hurt you more than I already have!"

"I love you Lexi," Julia starts, her eyes closed as if uttering a final prayer. "I'll see you soon, my love."

Julia strikes the match, and the sound of Officer Scott's gun going off shakes the walls. Julia topples to the floor, the lit match flinging from her fingers, and I watch it fall in what feels like slow motion until it connects with the floor and the blaze begins to spread.

"Everyone out, now!" Officer Scott yells through the smoke already collecting overhead.

In a matter of seconds, the flames have spread up the wall with no sign of stopping. I fall to the floor and begin crawling on my hands and knees, desperately trying to stay below the choking cloud. The floor is hot against my palms as I scurry along the floor, keeping my eyes locked on the exit. I can hear the others shouting orders to one another behind me, but the fire roaring around us makes their words indiscernible.

I want to look back, but between the blisters forming on my hands and the smoke beginning to fill my lungs, it's now or never. Footsteps thud behind me, gaining momentum, until they are sprinting past me. I look up to see Claire and Anna, supporting Sean on either side, and Jackson following shortly behind, his hand still clutching where the bullet struck him. I stand from the floor, ignoring the blisters and splinters that now cover my hands, and *run*.

I make it to the bottom of the stairs just outside the entryway before my body collapses to the ground.

In a matter of seconds, I'm being lifted from my crumpled heap and ushered to the nearest ambulance.

They run a number of tests, poking and prodding. I think they're asking me questions, but I can't really tell. The world around me sounds as though my ears have been padded off, reducing their words to incoherent murmurs.

"Somebody help me!" a voice shouts, followed by a fit of coughing.

I lift my head, the scene before me blurring in and out of focus. There's a group of people darting for the entrance, where Officer Scott has emerged from the smoke holding Julia, who lies limp in his arms.

I turn to my left to see Jackson step into the back of another ambulance with the assistance of Anna and Claire.

"Is he going to be okay?" Anna asks as they lay him back onto the table, strapping him in for transport to the hospital. Anna and Claire jump into the back of the truck, closing the door behind them before being driven away.

Julia is being loaded in the back of the third ambulance

on a stretcher. There's a mask attached to her face, which tells me she's breathing. A couple of medics begin assessing Officer Scott for anything that would require medical attention, but he waves them off, jumping inside and taking his place next to his daughter.

As the clean air replaces the smoke in my lungs, I lurch forward, pressing my face into my sleeve, the faded blue fabric speckled with gray and smelling of ash. I feel a hand pressing against my back and look up to see one of the EMTs, a younger-looking woman with her dark brown hair in a tight bun on her head.

"It's okay, sweetheart. It's all over now. You're safe."

I begin to sob as her words sink into my very bones. She's right. It's all over now. This will all become a distant memory, left behind in the ashes of Rosie's Diner.

Breathe in. Breathe out. I think to myself.

It's all over.

CHAPTER
THIRTY-TWO

LOGAN

The strong smell of brewed coffee and fresh-baked pastries rushes to my nose. I spot my fellow survivors sitting in the corner, basking in the morning sun that shines through the tall windows.

Claire gives a frantic wave, prompting Anna and Jackson to greet me with sleepy smiles. I order my coffee and an everything bagel with cream cheese before sitting in the empty chair next to Claire. Anna is snuggled up next to Jackson, careful not to jostle the arm that now rests in a sling across his body.

This is our first time all being in the same room since the hospital. Claire and I would pop in occasionally to check in on Jackson's recovery, but Anna never left his side. Every time we would arrive with homework assignments and a bag full of takeout in tow, she would be there. Always in the same spot next to Jackson's bed.

I suppose all of their down time forced Anna and Jackson to confront their demons head-on. Looking at them now across the small table, they have never looked happier. Claire hasn't changed much. She's still the bubbly person I met the night of my initiation, only now there's an air of confidence about her. Her shoulders are more relaxed, and I sense a certain peace.

"Caught up on all that homework?" Claire asks Jackson with a giggle.

"Almost. Only three more papers to turn in, and I'm all caught up."

"Only three?" Anna laughs, leaning her head on Jackson's good shoulder.

"Better than the ten I started with."

Looking around at the group, I am struck with inspiration. I pull my laptop from my bag, placing it on the table before me.

"Oh, are you finally ready to write that book?" Claire asks, giddy with excitement.

"I think so," I say with a nod.

Since the fire at Rosie's Diner, I've tried starting this story three separate times, but the beginning never felt right. Sitting here among my fellow survivors, seeing how strong they remain in the face of what's happened, I couldn't be more inspired.

"Don't paint me as too much of a bitch." Anna smiles, wagging her finger over the table.

"I'll do what I can," I reply, and the table bursts into laughter.

I open my laptop and take in the world around me. The smells, the sounds, the joy. I want to remember this moment exactly as it is for the rest of my life. We've been given a second chance at life, and I don't think any of us intend to waste it.

I stare at the blank page, the blinking cursor enticing me to begin. Blank pages are always intimidating, but the boundless power and possibilities it holds make it worth trying anyway. Wherever my dad is, I hope he is looking down on me. Today, I will embark on the final leg of the journey that he started all those years ago. Sharing in his mission to show how hurt can impact action.

I shove my arms into my dad's blue sweater, the same sweater he wore as he wrote his own stories. I zip it up, the fabric enveloping me in a warm embrace. Looking around the table one last time, I take a deep breath—and I start writing.

EPILOGUE
DOROTHY CLARK

THE NIGHT OF THE FIRE

Tears fill my eyes as I watch Logan pull away from the curb. He didn't say where he was going or why he was in such a rush, but I know something is wrong. A mother just knows these things.

Every fiber of me wanted to stop him. Shield him from the dangers lurking in this world. But I knew that it would be of no use. My baby boy is all grown up, and I have to let him face the world on his own. I have to let him go.

There are some things, however, that one can't let go of. While I can no longer physically protect my son, I can still protect him in other, thankless ways. Not thankless because Logan is ungrateful, not at all. But thankless because he doesn't know what I know.

As Logan turns off of our street, I retreat back into the house. I lock the door against the cold night and take in the room.

The house is silent—something I'm still getting used to.

When Logan was little and his father was still alive, I would come home after a long day to toys thrown about the living room and the TV blasting cartoons. Music would be playing from my husband's office, where I would usually find Logan scribbling the few words he knew how to spell on a notepad while his father typed away at his computer.

It was chaos, but it was *my* chaos.

At the time, I'm sure I would have given my right arm to come home to a tidy house, but these days, there's nothing I wouldn't give to clean up one more mess.

I move through the house until I'm standing in my late husband's office. His large oak desk looks just the same as the day he passed. I come in here occasionally to mop and dust the books and furniture. If I close my eyes, I can still hear the clacking of a keyboard or the whirring of a printer.

I stop in front of the bookshelf and find the first book my husband ever published. I pull it from its place until I hear the tell-tale click and the shelf pulls away from the wall on a set of hidden hinges.

Mounted to the wall behind the shelf is a safe where Logan's father and I would keep all sorts of things. Birth certificates, mortgage documents, and most recently—secrets.

I turn the knob, carefully placing the arrow on each number of the combination. The handle *thunks* as I grip it, and the door of the safe creaks open. I pull a small cardboard box from the safe and place it on the desk.

Removing the lid, I inspect the contents, feeling a pang in my chest as I'm transported to the night I almost lost my son forever.

Logan, like his father, is a creature of habit. Every

morning around eight, my boy would start a pot of coffee and pour himself a bowl of cereal. I would wake to the sound of the TV on in the living room and the smell of fresh coffee thick in the air.

The morning after his accident, I knew from the moment I opened my eyes that something was wrong. The living room was silent, there was no smell of coffee, and my son was nowhere to be found.

Through the window, I could see that my husband's car was missing, and that was when it hit me. I darted back to my bedroom, lifted my phone from the night stand, and saw that I had missed a call. With one tap, I was on the phone with a staff member from Westview Memorial Hospital, telling me that my son had been in an accident.

Is he alive? The thought passes in a flash.

Those were the first words I spoke that morning.

Before I left for the hospital, I grabbed a couple of things from Logan's room. His laptop, his headphones. The sound of something crunching underfoot drew my attention to the floor—and I saw them.

Small white ovals scattered across the floor next to an empty orange pill bottle. I lifted the bottle and recognized it from an operation I'd undergone the year before.

Painkillers make me horribly nauseous, so I'd put the bottle in the medicine cabinet hanging above the bathroom sink.

Something had told me to throw them away that day, but I kept them in case the ibuprofen I took instead wasn't strong enough.

When I saw the medication haphazardly strewn about my son's bedroom, everything clicked. A heaviness formed in my gut, and I swallowed back the tears that rushed to my eyes.

"My sweet Logan," I whispered to the stagnant air. "What have you done?"

I arrived at the hospital soon after, holding my breath as I entered the main lobby. I just needed someone, anyone, to tell me that my boy was okay. When I reached the emergency wing, there were two officers sitting in the waiting area. I must have looked as disheveled as I felt, because the taller one with the mustache started walking toward me.

"Are you Mrs. Clark?" he asked.

"Is Logan okay?" I skipped the pleasantries.

"Yes, he's fine," the other officer chimed in. "They just got him in a room, but we would like to ask you a couple of questions before you see him."

I nodded, agreeing to their terms, and we took our place in the three beige chairs in the corner of the room.

"Now, Mrs. Clark, we are hoping you can help us set a timeline for the incident last night," Mustache Man said.

I took note of the word "incident." So similar to "accident," but the two held very different meanings. Accident would have implied that this was a freak chance and it could have happened to anybody. Incident implied something much worse.

"I'll help however I can," I replied.

———

By the end of the questioning, I had learned three very important things: the other person involved in Logan's incident had not survived, their blood work had led them to believe that the other party was at fault, and my son had been hanging upside down for at least six hours before first responders arrived. The only thing that was up in the air was whether or not Lexi Pruitt was alive or not at the time of the crash. I answered each of their questions, preparing to somehow explain away the pills. Every answer I could come up with only painted me as a horrible mother. I decided at that moment that if I had to take the fall for all of this, I was willing to do it. I would have given my life, if it meant that my son could walk free.

Lucky for me, it never came to that. At the end of the questioning, the police escorted me to the room where my son was. I ran to him, kissing his sleeping face over and over. All of the tears I had been holding back since that morning flooded to the surface.

"We'll give you your space," Mustache Man said from the doorway, "If we need anything else, we will give you a call."

They walked out of that room and never came back.

I grew tired of waiting to be taken away, so I took some of the money Leonard left behind for us to hire a private investigator. Gerald was great at his job, and within a few days, I had the coroner report for Lexi sealed and delivered to my front door in a yellow envelope.

That was the day I discovered that Lexi had been alive at the time of impact, and in the end, it was the crash that ripped her life away from her.

———

Standing in my husband's office, a shiver slides down my spine. I twirl the bottle of pills in my hand, small white ovals dancing behind orange plastic. How can so much pain, fear, and guilt be tied to something so small?

I tuck the bottle into the cardboard box and return it to the safe. The bookcase closes, concealing the safe behind it once more. Before I step out of the office, I turn, gazing at the shelf where my husband's books are displayed.

Each speaks of someone who has been classified as a murderer in some capacity. Stories about ordinary people placed under horrible circumstances, who, in the moment, did the only thing they could do to break free.

Logan had such immense pain after the passing of his father that he did the only thing he could to rid himself of it. In trying to take away his pain, he only caused more.

I pray every day that my son never remembers what he tried to do that night. I pray that I never have to look him in the eyes and tell him that I kept such a thing from him. He would never forgive me, but he's my son, and I would do *anything* to protect him.

Anything to keep society from placing a label on my son without ever knowing him. To keep them from pointing their fingers and calling him a *murderer*, when he's never been violent a day in his life. He was a kid experiencing real loss for the first time, and he simply couldn't cope.

As his mother, I choose to take this burden from him. As long as I'm alive, Logan will never know that, in the end, he is the one who killed Lexi Pruitt.

ACKNOWLEDGMENTS

I'm not quite sure how to find the words to express all of the feelings I have surrounding the publication of my first novel, but I am sure going to try my best.

This idea was originally conceived when Britt, a close friend of mine, asked me if I would want to co-write something with her. She is a fantastic digital artist and we wanted to have a fun little academia adventure comic where I would write the story and she would transfer that into digital comic form!

With most things I write, I somehow found a way to make it quite dark, and eventually we came to the consensus together that our styles may not exactly lend themselves to one another. I asked her if I could continue to write this story we had started together. She gave me her blessing, and the rest is history.

I tried many times to write this book (four times to be exact), and with each attempt, I felt I was getting closer and closer to the story I wanted to tell.

At its core, *The Ghost Writers Club* is a story about navigating the ugly parts of loss and the pressures of living up to someone else'e legacy. It calls out a society that is so quick to pass judgment on someone based on labels without ever truly getting to know them. It challenges the morality of doing something society says is unredeemable

— like murder — when one feels they have no other options.

I wanted to make each of the characters someone that you could relate to in one way or another. None of them are perfect by any means, and ALL of them have made some pretty questionable decisions in their life. I wanted to highlight these poor choices, but share them in a way that a reader would think, "I would probably have done the same thing if I were in their position."

There are MANY people that helped make this story what it is today, and I would be remiss if I didn't take the time to mention them here.

Firstly, I want to thank my partner, Clark, for his unwavering support. Writing a book takes a lot of time. He has heard every idea and thought I had with this story (and trust me, I had a lot of ideas) and he never complained once. He would listen to me hash and rehash a scene out loud until it clicked into place, and his support was a HUGE asset in helping me finish this book.

Next, I want to thank my friend and neighbor, Robbie, who read the very first pages of this story while I was drafting it! Her feedback and encouragement on those early pages was crucial in the making of this story. It was also an extra bit of motivation to keep writing, because occasionally she would text me, wondering why I hadn't sent her a new chapter in days. LOL

This book went through many rounds of revision and along the way, I had the opportunity to work with some fantastic beta readers throughout the process. Alyssa, Sylvia, Penny, Ryan, Rebecca, Taylor, and Stephen, thank YOU for being the best writing friends a guy could ask for. Your feedback and encouragement helped me to hone my craft throughout this process, and this book truly wouldn't be what it is without you! <3

I want to send a huge shoutout to Christian Storm, my cover designer, for bringing the vision I had in my head to life. This cover is vibrant, eerie, and everything I could have ever imagined! I also want to shoutout Dylan Garrity for his work as my editor. His expertise taught me how to refine the things I wanted to say so that they had the impact I intended, and through working with him, I have added so many tools to my writer toolbox to use in future works!

Lastly, I want to thank all of YOU that followed my journey on YouTube. You left encouraging comments, provided me a sense of community, and made the process of writing this book such a joyful one. Often times, people would leave comments on my page, telling me that I was inspiring them, but what they didn't know was that it was truly them who fueled my inspiration. I will never find the words to thank you enough.

I want my last words in this book to be a note of encouragement to all of you that have toyed with the idea of writing your own book. Writing in itself is such a messy process at times. Your brain is flooded with ideas constantly, and you have to somehow find a way to organize them to create a cohesive story. It is difficult, time-consuming, and (sometimes) stressful. But it is also beautiful, healing, and powerful. If I had to make the decision to write this book all over again, I would do it in a heartbeat!

I put so much of myself in this story and it has seen me through some of the darkest moments of my life. I hope that reading this book provides you with a sense of hope that you can do anything you set your mind to.

The world needs your story. So it's time to start writing it!

With immense love,
   Cody <3